LIFE IN MOTION
HITCHHIKING THE UNITED STATES AND CANADA

BY MICHAEL MCCULLOUGH

Published by Starry Night Publishing.Com
Rochester, New York

D1714735

Michael McCullough

Dedicated to family and friends who encouraged me to keep writing, provided feedback, and read many drafts of the book.

This is a work of fiction based on true events from my life. I have tried to recreate events, locales, and conversations from my memories of them. In order to maintain their anonymity, I have changed the names of individuals, and in some cases made them up entirely from my imagination. It's possible some identifying characteristics and details such as physical properties, occupations, and places of residence have been altered.

"Would you tell me, please, which way I ought to go from here?" "That depends a good deal on where you want to get to," said the Cat. "I don't much care where," said Alice. "Then it doesn't matter which way you go," said the Cat. "-so long as I get somewhere, "Alice added as an explanation. "Oh, you're sure to do that," said the Cat, "if you only walk long enough." (Carroll, 71-72).[1]

[1] Carroll, Lewis. *Alice's Adventures in Wonderland*. MacMillan & Company. 1865

Contents

Introduction

    "Sean Matheson," said Mr. Flynn from across the room, "how can someone as young as you be so cynical? Trust me, everything will be okay, you need to stop worrying so much." Mr. Flynn was one of my favorite high school teachers. He towered over most of us, at least six foot four, had greasy or Brylcreem filled black hair that he would rub his hands through during lectures, he was old, at least forty-five, and was always calm in the classroom, which helped me focus. He would intersperse stories to make history come alive and tell them while leaning against the heat vents near the windows or strolling up and down the classroom aisles. Some teachers would degrade a student for a wrong answer, so I learned to keep my mouth shut. In Mr. Flynn's class I felt safe to respond to questions, knowing if I was wrong or disagreed with his opinion he would chide me, but in a kidding way, the feedback was never a putdown or trying to make a student feel inferior, or to put him in his place.

    This day's eleventh grade social studies lecture was a discussion on President Nixon's diplomatic negotiations with China. It was the spring of 1973 and the Watergate Scandal was coming to light. Didn't Mr. Flynn listen to the nightly news with Walter Cronkite? How could I not be cynical? Most of my childhood during the 1960's was spent watching the Vietnam War on television with a new body count every night, the country had endured race riots, President Kennedy was assassinated and died on my seventh birthday, my birthday for Christ's sake! We were sent home early from school that day and I entered the house with the television on and my Mom crying. It was a memory that burned into my soul and I was supposed to not be cynical?

    Assassinations of Martin Luther King and Robert Kennedy, protests in the streets against the war, college students in my hometown were even marching. Charles Manson ran loose killing people and I watched and read about it all before I even made it to high school. My family had the *Times-Union* newspaper delivered every day and I read it front to back. What pre-teen kid does that? Me. I read any magazine I could get my hands on: *The Saturday Evening Post, National Geographic, Time, Look, MAD Magazine,*

Reader's Digest, Sports Illustrated, really any I could find in the house or at the doctor or dentist offices. Those magazines were between the comic books, biographies, sports, history, and science fiction books I read non-stop. I couldn't go anywhere without a book in my hands. The local public library was one of my favorite places to visit. Of course cynicism ran through the core of my body and brain. The world was a mess and I didn't know how to fix it.

There were a few bright spots I could hang onto; dreams of what I might be able to become as an adult: Apollo missions - At age twelve I was sure to become an astronaut, it's why I built models of the LEM and Saturn rockets; playing and watching sports of all types, dreaming of becoming a professional football player, I knew the Baltimore Colts needed me on defense; exploring my neighborhood, the streets, the woods, old cemeteries, roaming everywhere I could, sometimes miles from my home even as a pre-teen and dreaming of traveling the world; being fascinated by old buildings and homes in our village, thinking I would become an architect as I spent hours designing my own houses; reading fiction books, writers like Ray Bradbury, Jack London, J.R.R. Tolkien, and Jules Verne, there were so many stories in my head I was sure to become a writer; watching Jacques Cousteau's Undersea World documentaries on television, I was always drawn to water, why not become an oceanographer?

If you let someone control your life who knows how it will turn out? Growing up and maturing is a long journey with many starts and stops, taking you to places you couldn't dream of with new opportunities presenting themselves at the most unlikely times. Love comes and goes with often disastrous results, especially if you are a male who feels things too deeply. Crying, expressing heartfelt emotions are not what a real man does, at least that was the lesson I learned over and over again in my family, so maybe he participates in activities that many people would consider reckless? He cannot see the road ending, or if it does, it does so quickly. So what? Live today, worry about tomorrow as if it will never come.

"I shall be telling this with a sigh
Somewhere ages and ages hence:
Two roads diverged in a wood, and I,
I took the one less traveled by,
And that has made all the difference." (Frost, Robert Lee) [2]

[2] Frost, Robert Lee. *The Road Less Taken.* n.p. 1915

Michael McCullough

The Barge Inn

Ben was one of my best friends since junior high. Well, there was that time I pushed him up against the windows in the school cafeteria in front of a couple of hundred students for making fun of me, and for some stupid reason I began punching him before the teachers on lunch duty broke us up. Tonight, though, he was nursing his third rum and Coke while I worked on my fourth or fifth black Russian, who could count at this point? We sat at a booth across from the bar while the jukebox was blasting out the Doobie Brothers "Black Water" for the third time that night. The Barge Inn had become my second home a couple of months after I turned eighteen in November of 1974. I had dropped out of Brockport State before the start of the spring semester, in part because I was confused about what to study in college. At eighteen how was I supposed to know what I wanted to be in life? In my mind everyone around me seemed to know what they were doing, I sure didn't.

Adding to the inner turmoil, around Christmas time a girl I had been dating suddenly, and unexpectedly, dumped me, with no explanation as to why. After that experience drinking and getting high were the best activities I could come up with, except for some pickup basketball games at the college. Even the job I had working at the college bookstore in the fall had to go by the wayside, the requirement was to be a student to work part-time at the store. That was probably for the best since my ex's mother worked at the bookstore and seeing her, made me think of her daughter. But the loss of an income and some kind of identity hurt. My closest friends were still in college, I was suddenly an outsider.

And I was lost.

Ben kept trying to come up with good opening lines to use on picking up one of the chicks hanging out in the bar and maybe score a one-nighter, but with his barely intelligible slurring of words I was pretty sure nothing was going to work. It was getting near closing time and when you've been at the bar since six p.m. for the last part of happy hour, six Old Vienna Splits for a dollar (which was two hours if you knew the right bartender... and we did) all reality is subject to wild interpretation. Earlier I had been able to hustle a couple of oafs at the pool table. Even when drunk I could shoot a mean game of eight ball and earn enough cash for a couple of more rounds of drinks.

Turns out we had a great viewing angle to the start of this episode of Saturday night fights. A friend from high school, Paul Davis, seemed to relish getting into fights in the local bars. Paul had been a teammate of mine on our high school football team, was an All-County wrestler, and had made the football team at Davidson College in North Carolina as a backup center his freshman year. Paul had come home from college during a long weekend break. Crowded nights at the Barge Inn the wrong person would accidentally bump into Paul and all hell would break loose. High School, now college friends of ours, Wayne and Jeff, were all too happy to participate. This night a war of words between townies Paul, Wayne, Jeff and four nut jobs from the dorms quickly escalated into a shoving match and then punching.

Part of my brain said to join in, tackle someone, anyone, and begin punching, but the few sober brain cells left in my head realized it would end up badly for me. I barely made it back from the bar with our last round of drinks without spilling them, throwing a punch was out of the question. It seemed the trio could handle themselves at this point, and besides, who wanted the possibility of ending up on the mangy bar floor that was covered in booze, cigarette butts, and dirt? An instant later Scott, our favorite bartender and a friend from high school, climbed over the bar past the blonde coed he had been plying with free drinks in hopes of getting lucky, and joined the fray.

Paul was in a bad spot, taking a beating from some ape who had him pinned against a table and was biting his lip, and not in a good way. Paul managed to pick up an empty Pabst beer bottle and smash it on the guy's head several times, breaking the bottle and making blood flow from his scalp. This sufficiently stunned his attacker and I just watched like it was a saloon fight from an old episode of "*Gunsmoke*" and calmly sipped my drink, frozen in time. Paul hammered the guy's ribs with a couple of rights and finally put him on the floor before the bouncers pushed through the crowd with two of Brockport's finest and hauled both of them to the hospital. Scott went back behind the bar, Jeff, Wayne, and the other fight participants sank into the crowd, eventually going out the rear emergency door, disappearing into the night like nothing had happened.

As Ben and I staggered to my brown 1969 Dodge Coronet, we saw Jeff helping a shoulder length, brown-haired coed into the passenger seat of his van, a typical Saturday night for him. We left Scott in the bar, not sure if the blonde girl he was feeding tequila drinks to was going to make his night a happy one.

We heard the next day that the winner by stitch count was Paul, with eight on his lip compared to twelve on the other guy's scalp. The emergency room doctor assured Paul his lip would heal without a scar, but it would be a couple of weeks before any kissing could resume, and eating would be a bit tough without drooling.

Michael McCullough

Weighted Down

Still feeling lost and like my life had been blown off course after missing a semester of classes, I decided to register at Brockport State for the fall of 1975. I had no desire to work full-time at a factory like Kodak, joining the military wasn't a popular option so soon after the Vietnam War had ended, so all I could come up with was college. Why I decided to go back to Brockport State and face three or more years of uncertainty instead of trying a community college was a bit baffling, but at least I could walk to campus and the bars from home. Beginning in late spring and continuing through the summer months I practiced tennis every day, playing anyone who would show up at the courts, hitting hundreds of serves from every side of the court, hitting balls against a wall for hours, running sprints, and even managed to cut way back on my partying, getting smashed two nights a week instead of five or more. Also, fortunately, I was able to get my job back at the college bookstore starting a couple of weeks before the semester. I learned to block out seeing my ex's mother.

Tennis gave me a goal, gave my life a tiny bit of direction. Unfortunately, despite my dedication to training, I got cut from the college tennis team. It turned out they were one of the best teams in the SUNY system and only kept fourteen players, most of whom had returned from the previous season. There was no freshman team, so I found solace getting high and drunk the next several nights to soothe my disappointment. My time was now spent attending classes sporadically, with the usual going through the motions attempts at studying, working at the college bookstore, which was a job I actually enjoyed, partying, playing pickup basketball games (why go to my night class, accounting, which I hated and didn't understand, when I could play basketball?) intramural football, and the weight room.

Paul had transferred to SUNY Brockport from Davidson College in North Carolina after his freshman year. He wanted to be closer to home and had a better opportunity to be a starter on the football team at Brockport than Davidson. During the football season I spent a lot of time in the weight room and after it ended I joined him and a few other friends for two to three hour sessions several days a week in the late afternoons or early evenings. The workouts were a great escape from life and made me begin thinking about bulking up to go out for the football team the next year. At six feet one my height was decent, but a slim one-hundred sixty-five pounds wasn't going to cut it as a college offensive guard or defensive end, no matter how quick I was.

By February, after four months of hard work, eating and drinking everything in sight, mixing protein powder into a gallon of milk every day, my weight had gone up a measly ten pounds. You'd think my partying would have put weight on all by itself, but I just burned all the calories off. I could bench press seventy pounds more than my body weight, not bad, and actually saw real biceps on my body, but still...not college football offensive guard or defensive end material, and I wasn't much good at catching or throwing passes, so my confidence was fading. Tennis could still have been an option, but not having money to join a private club during the winter meant no practice time for months. I lost interest in pursuing the dream of making any college team and worked out only because I loved it. My body felt alive in the gym or on a basketball or tennis court. I needed to move even if I was a pretty average athlete.

One night in the weight room there was a guy working over the heavy punching bag. He was short, maybe five feet six, but with Popeye forearms and tree trunk thighs. Sweat was streaming down his face and his loose grey shirt with frayed arm sleeves was soaked. I had learned a bit about boxing in high school from Mr. Fleming, our physical education teacher. He encouraged me, and probably all of his students, to play sports. I always stayed after school for intramurals, whether volleyball, gymnastics, basketball, or weightlifting, it didn't matter, I tried them all. I wasn't really good at any of them, I just loved moving. The gym was my safe spot in school. One day I asked Mr. Fleming to teach me about using the heavy punching bag that was hanging in the equipment room in-between wrestling mats, the parallel bars, baskets of volleyballs and dodge balls. I never saw any other student use the bag. Mr. Fleming would sign passes for me to come down from study hall to work out on the bag. After school he taught me how to combine jabs, crosses, hooks and gave me a small poster so I knew what to keep working on. I liked being alone in the room as Mr. Fleming went off to teach a class. He trusted me to do the right thing, not bother anyone or any equipment, and so it was just me and the bag, the sound of my gloves pop-popping on the leather, sweat dripping from my brow, pretending I was punching out a bully or teacher who had pissed me off, at the same time I was learning to defend myself and keep my body moving. The workouts helped me stay in shape and out of trouble. Maybe I should have been in study hall reading one of my textbooks, but this was so much more fun. I went back to class stinking of body odor and had sweat dripping from my head, but I didn't care. Between my acne and inability to talk to any girl I had an interest in dating, body odor was the least of my concerns. During the day it seemed like I always had to keep moving until finally late at night I would be too exhausted to do anything else but lie down, watch the "*Six Million Dollar Man*" or some other television show, or read a Ray Bradbury book and fall asleep.

I walked over to watch Popeye Junior in the weight room and when he finished his practice round asked if I could jump in.

"Without gloves?" he asked. "That would be stupid. You'd cut your hands to shreds."

"Where do I get a pair from, do they loan them in the equipment room?" I replied.

"No, meet me here tomorrow around six p.m. I have an old pair I'll sell you for five bucks, then I'll show you a few things on the bag okay?"

"That sounds great, hey, what's your name?" I asked.

"Jason."

With that I had the rest of my spring semester days settled: classes, studying, the bookstore job, weights, and now, boxing. I even liked my classes: two political science courses, American literature, astronomy, introduction to geology, and somehow was earning passing grades in all of them!

I met with Jason at least once a week over the next three months, learning more combinations, how to shadow box effectively, and even sparring with him a few times. Jason always kicked the crap out of me sparring, despite the height differences, but it was still fun. I didn't care about the bruises on my ribs or

17

occasional red marks on my cheeks I'd find at home when showering. I learned more than what Mr. Fleming had time to teach me and always added a heavy bag workout at the end of my weight training sessions. I was in shape, even if it wasn't football shape. The month of May and the end of the semester came too soon.

Last Call for Alcohol

Sticky floors, a smoky haze permeating the air, the slight smell of stale beer, glass and bottle stains on the tables and bar top, I could be blindfolded and know I was in my second home, the Barge Inn. It was an early June Saturday night. I was still searching for a summer job to pay for next semester's tuition and books. I wasn't able to stay working at the college bookstore over the summer and was having difficulty finding somewhere else to work, or maybe was too picky to take whatever junky job I could find. I'd been slamming drinks and playing pool since seven p.m., typical behavior for me, and feeling fine at midnight. All the usual suspects were here, Paul, Chuck, Todd, Jeff, Mike, Tom, Wayne, former high school and now college friends, hanging out shooting the shit and drinking. The jukebox was cranking out Steve Miller's "The Joker" when Paul pulled me up to the bar.

"I'm headin' to California, then up the coast to Seattle to visit my grandparents, going into Canada and back home," he said, slurring his words.

"C'mon, are you serious?" I asked. "How are you getting out there without a car?"

"Hitchhike of course," he replied. "It won't be a problem; I've got the route all planned, leave from Brockport, take Interstate 90 as much as possible to Yellowstone National Park, then weave my way over to Big Sur in California, up the coast to Seattle and Highway 1 across Canada. The Olympics are in Montreal this summer so rides up there should be easy to get."

"The only hitchhiking we've done is around here, maybe fifteen miles or so, you sure a what, 5,500 mile trip is a good thing to attempt?" I wondered.

"Nah, it'll be no problem, I've made it to Buffalo and back a few times, that's a hundred miles round trip. Remember that girl I dated, Becky? I hitched rides to her house and back a few weekends during early spring until she dumped my ass."

"Too bad I still don't have my Dodge," I said. "That would have been a nice car to cruise the country in."

"Why did you get rid of that, what happened again?" Paul asked.

"You were at Davidson College when I dropped out before the spring semester of '75, had no money, couldn't work at the bookstore anymore since you had to be a student, and the car had some mechanical problems, maybe due to me not thinking about adding oil on a regular basis. What the hell did I know about engines? That was my brother's gig, I was a mechanical idiot. You put gas in the tank, turned the key in the ignition and drove. Simple, right? No, apparently, and one day the Dodge just stopped working."

I took a drink before continuing, "Dad didn't like my car sitting in his driveway, thought it was blocking him from getting out of the garage. A freaking double wide driveway and he couldn't get out. What the hell. Maybe the old man needed a refresher course in driving a car. So instead of loaning me some cash so I could get the Dodge fixed, maybe be able to use it to get a job and commute back and forth to work, he said I had to sell it. I stayed pissed about that for a long time, thinking about it, I guess I'm still pissed at him. I bought the car with my own money and had some good times with it. Remember? I could fit a lot of people in it and the back seat was nice for making out, though I haven't done that for a long time. I should have stood up to him and argued, but it wasn't a good time for me, my head was a mess. On the plus side the cash from the sale gave me drinking money for a few months."

"Oh yeah, man you did learn how to drink during that time! Whenever I came home from Davidson you were out of control, not that you are much better now," joked Paul.

"I have a reputation to keep up now and drinking is something I'm good at. Anyhow, what if I join you on this adventure, maybe keep you company?" I asked. While Paul considered this idea I put a quarter in the jukebox and chose the perfect song by Lynyrd Skynyrd, "Call Me the Breeze".

The bell for last call rang, so I bought us another round, gin and tonic for him, black Russian for me, while he considered my offer.

"That's not a bad idea, it might be nice to have some company," said Paul. "But aren't you worried about what your parents will say?"

I took a sip of my drink, "Not really, I'm nineteen, not much they can really do to stop me. Think of what Jack London wrote, 'The proper function of a man is to live, not just to exist. I shall not waste my days trying to prolong them.'[3] (London vii).

"The only London I've read is *Call of the Wild*, so I don't know about living by that motto, but whatever," said Paul.

"Maybe I just don't care," I said. "I've certainly done enough other crazy things already so this shouldn't come as too much of a surprise. It'll make up for my Dad making me sell my car. I'm pretty good at pissing him off by doing the opposite of what he says, why not take a cheap vacation hitchhiking?"

"Hey, well, great, then it's settled. We leave in two weeks, on Sunday the twenty-seventh, so get your gear packed. What is that stupid name you call your backpack, Atlas? Yeah, figure out what you want in Atlas and how you are breaking the news to Mom and Dad."

With that we raised our glasses, yelled "Cheers" and downed our drinks.

[3] London, Jack. Call of the Wild and Other Stories. Dodd, Mead & Company. 1960.

Michael McCullough

Atlas

I was not going to hitchhike across the country without my brown Jansport backpack. One of my biggest purchases ever, at forty dollars, it had already served me well. The pack offered space at the top of the frame for a sleeping bag, space below the main storage area for a tent and ground cover, zippered pockets, it was lightweight, and was easy to overload with too much weight and too much gear. It had bars that curled around my waist making carrying it much more comfortable and kept the pack upright when it was placed on the ground. I liked the pack so much that I named it Atlas; the god of strength and heavy burdens, holding the weight of my belongings, books, and any necessary maps.

The pack had already accompanied me on long multi-day hikes in the Allegheny National Forest in Pennsylvania, the Presidential Range in the White Mountains of New Hampshire, and the Finger Lakes National Forest near Seneca Lake in New York. I figured the backpack would be the least of my issues heading across America and back home through Canada.

In my usual anal-retentive fashion I made a list on paper of everything to pack two days before I began, and then laid it all out on my bedroom floor. Many items were absolute necessities: for the outside of the pack, my green Coleman two man tent, the aforementioned mummy sleeping bag, and a ground pad to sleep on. In the Allegheny Forest, hiking with Paul, I had refused to sleep in our two man tent, instead opting for lying under the stars even though the temperature had dropped below freezing on our early spring adventure. It was a silly experiment to try, but concern about my personal well-being had mostly disappeared during the past year. I crawled into the bag, wearing long cotton underwear, heavy socks, and a ski cap. I zipped the bag tight and curled up enough to keep all but the top of my head inside. The chilly night air didn't bother me a bit; fortunately no wild animals bothered me either. That's one reason why this bag and I were not going to be split up anytime soon.

In one of the four side-zippered pockets I had my wallet with thirty dollars in cash, my driver's license, a list of phone numbers, a couple of photographs of family, and, unknown to Paul, my Dad's BankAmericard. I didn't know how many cards he had, but was happy to carry this one along for emergencies and a bit shocked when he let me have it. Of course it came with a warning,

"Guard this card with your life and only use it in an absolute emergency. You'll have to pay me back, with interest, if you do use it, you know that, right?"

"Yeah, I know, thanks Dad. I'll bury it deep inside Atlas."

"Atlas, who the hell is that, what are you talking about?"

"My pack, I named it Atlas."

"You're a little strange, Sean. Just keep the damn card safe."

I also had two old film canisters, the kind we usually used for carrying pot but now had change inside for the phone booths. Paul and I had agreed this would not be a trip we would be carrying any drugs on, relying on the kindness of strangers for that.

A second small side pocket had my personal hygiene kit: toothbrush, toothpaste, a small hairbrush (since a comb didn't work on my almost shoulder length thick, somewhat curly, brown hair), a small bottle of biodegradable shampoo/soap, a small spray can of Mennen deodorant, a new bar of red Lifebuoy soap, a baggy filled with toilet paper, Gillette shaving cream, a razor, and extra blades. Another baggy carried six Trojan condoms, because you just never knew, or at least had to have hope that the time would come I might be able to put one to good use.

The third pocket had my Swiss Army knife (which I always found to be a marvel of innovation). Mine had two blades, small scissors, and nail file, can opener, bottle opener, two screwdrivers, and tweezers. The pocket also had a flashlight, Kodak Instamatic 110 camera and two extra film canisters, sunglasses, my General Electric AM/FM transistor radio with headphones, a blank journal, and two Parker 25 pens. The last side pocket had my first-aid supplies: Band-Aids of assorted sizes, tubes of Neosporin and Benadryl, Off! bug-repellent spray, Coppertone suntan lotion, matches, a Zippo lighter, and two folded paper road maps of the Interstate highway system; one for east of the Mississippi, one west.

I neglected a map of Canada and the Trans-Canada highway system, which would come back to haunt me. The main storage area on my pack had a small zippered pocket on the outside. I kept two paperback books in it that I had yet to read, *One Day in the Life of Ivan Denisovich* by Alexander Solzhenitsyn and *On the Road* by Jack Kerouac. I was probably the only hitchhiker who had his own copy of *The Elements of Style* tucked away. I figured it might come in handy when I was writing in my journal. Within easy reach was an emergency candy supply: one each of a Payday, Snickers, and Butterfinger bar. I wasn't a big chocolate eater, a heavy case of zits in high school cured that, but a taste once in a while seemed like an okay idea for a long trip.

The main compartment of Atlas had my black Adidas tennis sneakers, a pair of cheap sandals, a plastic bag for dirty clothes, a Ziploc baggie filled with Wisk powdered detergent, a yellow rain poncho, three pairs of socks, four pair of Jockey underwear (two white, two blue), two white undershirts, a pair of Oshkosh overalls, one pair of Levi jeans, a blue plaid flannel shirt, Long John underwear, a dark green "keep on truckin" t-shirt, a light green Brockport State earth science club shirt with gold lettering, a tie dye shirt, a black muscle shirt, navy blue gym shorts, a bath towel, and light brown pajama pants. At the bottom of the compartment was a baggie with Dad's credit card and another one hundred dollars in cash. I had a mess kit that included a pot, measuring cup, frying pan, and a baggie with a knife, fork, and spoon. I brought food that seemed essential: graham crackers, peanut butter, a can of tuna fish, three sleeves of Ritz crackers, a dozen gingersnap cookies in a Ziploc bag, a loaf of rye bread, and my own gorp mix creation - nuts, chocolate chips, granola, pretzels, and no fucking raisins. The outside hooks on Atlas had two canteens for water. I felt ready to travel. I laid out my clothes for our first morning: hiking boots, socks, underwear, cut-off jean shorts, my light blue Edgar Allen Poe t-shirt with a black raven on it, my Timex wrist watch, and a Rochester Red wing baseball hat.

Paul declined to discuss much about what was in his backpack. "And why would I name my pack?" he asked. "That's stupid; sometimes you're such a putz. Don't worry," he continued, "I brought plenty of food, including bananas and apples, I have to have my fruit. You should try eating healthier, Sean; it'd be good for you. I also made my own gorp, bags of it, except, unlike you, I believe in raisins in my gorp, hence the name, "good ol' raisins and peanuts"

Raisins, I just couldn't understand why any human would eat those wrinkled little deer turds. With that the planning and preparation for the adventure was done, Sunday, June 27, 1976, would be the beginning of our little jaunt across the country.

Land Cruiser

holding sign, WEST bound
thumbs out, optimism alive
on road out of here

My morning breakfast consisted of a bowl of Rice Krispies with milk and sliced banana before meeting up with Paul. He hugged his Mom and we walked the mile from our neighborhood in Brockport to the main road, Route 19, which would take us to the New York State Thruway. A warm summer sun gave us plenty of reason to be optimistic about our adventure.

Unbelievably, ten minutes after placing our backpacks on the shoulder of the road at 7:30 a.m., along came Richard Randall in his brand new red Toyota Land Cruiser. Richard, a friend of Paul's in the geology program who had graduated in late May, was on his way to a job at Yellowstone National Park in Wyoming. His parents had given him the Land Cruiser as a graduation gift and to help make the trip easier. Meanwhile, my parents were moving fifteen miles from campus in a few months and made me sell my car, so instead of walking or driving I'd have to borrow a car or hitchhike to school and work. Life wasn't always fair. I loved traveling and couldn't wait to move out of boring, dreary, snowy, Western New York, but while I was in college being able to walk the mile to campus or the bars was a decided advantage. Too soon that would be ending.

Richard's Cruiser was loaded down with clothes, a cooler, a backpack, two suitcases, hiking boots, camping equipment, a record player, speakers, and records, but he let us jam our backpacks on the rear bench seat next to me and Paul sat upfront. We were officially on our way west.

"I'm stopping in Chicago to visit my aunt and uncle for a couple of days before heading to Wyoming, so you two will have to get out and begin hitchhiking when I leave I-90 for their house." Richard said. "That'll still get you around six hundred miles from here, not a bad start."

I nodded my head in agreement and Paul thanked him again for giving us a ride. The two geology nerds started a conversation about Paul collecting rocks from every state we visited, which seemed a bit absurd to me and a lot of weight to carry around. I relaxed in the backseat, which actually was a bit uncomfortable, lacking in cushioning and leg room, and zoned out watching the scenery pass by. Interstate 90 through western New York was pretty flat, mostly just farmland, houses out in the distance, not even billboards to read and help pass the time. We had driven about forty miles, closing in on Buffalo, when Richard began whining about some noise he heard in his Toyota.

"Hey Sean, are you rattling something back there?" he asked, looking at me through the rearview mirror.

"No, I'm hanging out back here eating some graham crackers and listening to you two talk about rocks, but trying to ignore it at the same time," I said. "Let me check out our packs."

"You better not be dropping any crumbs in my truck!"

"Don't worry, I'm keeping it clean back here," I said, brushing the crumbs off my legs and onto the floor and without adding screw you to my sentence.

The packs seemed secure, everything I could see in the back behind my seat seemed secure, I didn't know what the dumb rich shit was hearing. I had a feeling this wasn't going to end well for Paul and me. From the time Richard picked us up I didn't get any warm and fuzzy feeling from him about us, just more of an obligation since he had relied on Paul during the semester to get him through a Mineralogy class. That was a tough subject with an even tougher, no nonsense professor. Accordingly, I opted out of that class, it was one reason I was considering a double major in earth science and English, I could study astronomy, anthropology, archeology, basic geology, meteorology, and an assortment of other subjects, but skip calculus, organic chemistry, and higher level intense geology classes.

"Well, it better not be my Cruiser making any noises," Richard said.

We kept on driving, through the toll gates near eastern Buffalo and then more a few miles south of Buffalo. New York had a way of sucking money from drivers even though the thruway was supposed to have been free to drive on ten years ago. Near Fredonia, New York, about fifty minutes south of Buffalo, Richard had had enough; the rattling was driving him nuts.

"I think it's the weight from you two and your pack," he said. "I'm going to have to drop you off here, it's near Fredonia State College, I'm sure you can get another ride quickly."

Really, a vehicle that can tow over 6,000 pounds and Paul, me, and our backpacks, maybe a combined weight of 450 pounds, are weighing down his precious cruiser? Asshat. Not to mention it was freaking summer, how many college kids would be traveling the last weekend of June?

Some things you only say in your head though, at least I do. It's especially fun being in my head during the middle of the night, when I wake up, think of three different things I should have said or done at an earlier time, maybe even years before, and then can't get back to sleep. So this time all I said was, "well, thanks for the ride Richard, we appreciate it, at least we're a couple of hours away from Brockport."

Paul and I took our backpacks from the cruiser, wished Richard a safe trip, and watched him drive off up the on-ramp and onto the Interstate.

"C'mon Paul, you know our body weight and backpacks weren't bothering his precious Land Cruiser, that thing is built to haul or tow thousands of pounds. Richard was being a dolt."

"Don't worry about it; we'll get another ride soon. It's a new truck, he's just being careful. Besides, he got us out of Brockport quickly. Who knows how long we could have been waiting there for a ride if not for him."

"Yeah, but it would have been nice to be all the way to Chicago by the end of the day."

"Suck it up."

With that we stuck out our thumbs, propped the WEST sign against Atlas, and hoped for the best.

Starry, Starry Night

I guess if you think about it, leaving Brockport before eight a.m. and being two hours' drive time away by 10:30 was probably a really good time when we were begging for rides. I wanted more though. We were still filled with a good amount of optimism, with a goal of making Yellowstone National Park in a week. Being left near Fredonia, a college town, didn't seem like the worst thing that could happen to us, even if Richard was being a jerk.

Paul and I forgot a prison was nearby and were thankful, as two state troopers drove past us, that we had stayed on the ramp instead of walking up to the main highway and been considered trespassers. While waiting for someone, anyone, to stop, we both ate some of our gorp, which I topped off with a few ginger snap cookies and a Payday bar. Paul kept his diet healthy by eating an apple and banana in his roadside lunch. When it took two hours before we were offered a ride, our optimism of making it a long way on our first day had faded.

An older, bald man with a grey handlebar mustache, driving a silver 1976 Ford Ltd with a Gannon University bumper sticker, stopped on the ramp, lowered his power side window, and said, "I'm heading to Erie if you boys want a ride. I'll open the trunk, put your packs in there and hop in the car."

Paul took shotgun and I was greeted at the rear door by a golden retriever wagging his tail and staring at my face.

"Don't mind Barkley, he's just being friendly. I think he's tired of having only me to ride with. Have a seat and I bet Barkley will lay his head on your lap. He's gotten pretty old and lazy like me."

Not sure I wanted a dog lying on my lap I was hesitant about sitting in the rear seat, but Paul had left me no choice, so I did as the driver told me to and buckled up in the seat next to the window. Barkley lay down and put his giant furry head on my leg. I could see his fur shedding onto my shorts, but began petting Barkley right away anyhow. Suddenly it got easy for me to get comfortable in the air-conditioned car that seemed to float down the Interstate.

"I'm Henry," said the driver as he reached out to shake Paul's hand. "And your names might be?"

"That's Sean in the back cuddled up with Barkley, I'm Paul. We left Brockport this morning and are heading to California, then Seattle to visit my grandparents, before coming back home."

"Quite a trip you have planned, I did some hitching of rides back in the day, but the longest was only to Erie a few times when I couldn't afford bus fare to get back to Gannon University from my home in Tonawanda."

"Why are you going to Erie now?" asked Paul.

"Oh, my wife and I live there, a few miles from our son, daughter-in-law, and two young grandchildren. I visited my parents in Tonawanda overnight and I'm just heading home. They're still doing pretty well for a couple of seventy-nine year olds."

Henry was friendly and kept up the conversation, mostly about his children and grandchildren, which was fine with me, I was happy just being out of the heat and heading toward the west coast. An hour later he dropped us off at the Peach Street exit to Erie near the on-ramp back to I-90. Barkley whined when I moved his head from my leg.

It was another two hours before we got a ride with a thirty-something year old pasty-faced guy dressed in a blue business suit and driving a maroon 1975 Dodge Monaco sedan. He had long brown hair in a Rod Stewart style cut. A half-smoked White Owl cigar was in the ashtray and I had to unroll the rear window to get fresh air flowing.

"Hurry up and get in, there's too much traffic to be standing around," he said. "I'm not sure and don't much care where you're going, I just want a bit of company while I'm driving back home to Willoughby Hills."

"Willoughby Hills? Where's that?" I asked.

"Ohio, about ninety minutes away."

"Sweet, we'll take it," said Paul. I sat in the back with our packs and Paul rode up front again.

It was a weird ride, with no sharing of names or talking. I just watched the flat land of western Pennsylvania and eastern Ohio and read billboards to pass time. The driver seemed fine with letting us sit there while he listened to an 8-track tape of Chicago's greatest hits, re-lit and slowly smoked his cigar. I'm not sure what company we actually provided him with, but I was fine sitting in the back and munching the rest of my gorp and a Butterfinger bar. He dropped us off at the exit ramp to Willoughby Hills with a quick wave and continued to his home.

It was past five p.m. and the day was taking a toll on us. Hitchhiking across the entire country and then thinking we could easily get back through Canada was beginning to seem like a daunting task to me and this was our first day! I wasn't sure what I expected, but this wasn't it. Maybe I should have bought a cheap used car and driven us around the country. We could have driven on any road we wanted, stopped where we wanted, and slept in the car if necessary. I was the one who asked to go on this trek though and had to suck it up and try and learn to go with the flow, or lack of a flow.

Thumbs out, packs by our sides, hot summer asphalt, cars and trucks flying by weaving toward us as if to plow us into the pavement or ditches, diesel fumes blowing at our faces and up our nostrils, cars teasing us by slowing down taking a look as if to offer a ride then speeding off when we began to step toward them, lit cigarettes thrown in our direction, middle fingers flying, screams of hippie or bum, it was easy to question why we were out here. Fighting boredom, having to pee, hungry but scared to dip too deep so soon into our food supply, holding our "WEST" sign, subject to the elements, wind, hot sun, hoping for one decent person to come along who needed company on their ride, who wanted to hear our story or tell theirs, this was now our life.

We stood on the ramp until nine p.m. before coming to the conclusion that another ride wasn't going to happen today.

"Let's get into the field over there for the night," Paul said, pointing to a spot off of Interstate 271 and I-90.

"I guess that's a reasonable idea," I said. "But we aren't raising the tent, it'll be us under the stars in our bags, we don't need to draw attention to ourselves so close to the highway."

"Yeah, I agree, let's try to make the best of it sleeping in the grass," replied Paul.

***

Ebony night sky

silence broken by crickets

stars mesmerizing

The stress of the day gave me a mental, rather than physical, beating. We ate some peanut butter on rye sandwiches and drank water from our canteens for dinner. We both slept in the clothes we had been wearing all day, except for the boots, of course. When we had to pee, we hid behind our packs and knelt down. After staring at Mars, Jupiter, picking out Scorpius, and Ursa Major and Minor, I fell asleep. Every hour or so I was awakened by trucks pulling out of the restaurant across the highway or from the nearby gas stations. I kept worrying that someone would walk across the field and yell at us.

At sunrise Paul made us do fifty push-ups and sit-ups. He was insistent in keeping us doing some kind of strength work and I just went along with it. I had changed into my tie-dye shirt, clean underwear, and socks. Paul changed into his Brockport State football shirt, cutoffs, and boots. We sprayed deodorant on our pits and privates before loading our packs on our backs and walking over to Mama Lucia's Family restaurant. Hank Williams' "Your Cheatin' Heart" was playing on the jukebox. It smelled like cigarette smoke, coffee, bacon, and grease. I noticed the waitress's name tag, Carol, and her yellowed teeth from smoking a few too many cigarettes, as she sat us at a booth and placed menus on the table. I looked up at the ceiling and the tiles were as yellow as Carol's teeth. She wasn't the friendliest person, at least not to us, maybe because of our backpacks; maybe because she saw us walking out of the field after sleeping there, or maybe we looked like hippies to her, I wasn't sure. Paul and I took turns using the bathroom, getting as clean as possible after a night in the weeds. I could feel, and see, from the truckers and others sitting around us, that we weren't exactly welcome. The customers seemed to be looking over at us or pointing their fingers in our direction. Maybe Mama didn't like strangers with long hair and backpacks in her place?

Paul ordered the Paul Bunyan breakfast special, two eggs, two pancakes, two bacon slices and two pieces of toast. He was still trying to keep his football weight on or else thought this was his last meal for the day. I went a bit lighter, with a short stack of buttermilk pancakes and a side of bacon. We shared an urn of coffee. For four dollars plus a tip we were stuffed. Even if the atmosphere was less than welcoming at least the food was good. During breakfast Paul pulled out and studied his road map while I wrote a few notes in my journal. We headed out to the highway by seven a.m. Watching the other restaurant customers; truckers heading toward their semis and commuters on the road looking at us like we were criminals, was unsettling, to say the least.

A semi-truck driver did offer a ride, but only for one passenger, he wasn't going to have two strangers sitting in his cab. We understood his view and there was a bit of temptation, but we weren't ready to split up. We waited another hour for a ride before Paul suggested,

"We aren't doing very well getting rides here, maybe we should switch, go down Interstate 271 and eventually over to Interstate 70 instead? We'll end up going through Columbus and Dayton, Ohio, over to Indianapolis, through St. Louis and Kansas City before arriving in Colorado. On I-90, if we could get a ride, we'd go through Cleveland, south of Chicago, Sioux Falls, Rapid City, and into Wyoming. We probably wouldn't see your friends in Windsor, Colorado if we took I-90, so this way we'll get an opportunity to visit with them. I-90 is a bit of a shorter, more direct route to Yellowstone, but I'm pretty frustrated sitting on the road with few rides. I have a good feeling about heading to I-70, even if it is a bit further."

"That seems a bit out of the way, but considering our lack of luck getting rides on I-90, it might be a good idea," I replied. "I'm okay with the change. What the hell, I've never been in that part of the country anyhow, let's go. Too bad your friend Richard couldn't have taken us a bit further."

"Forget about him, okay, we'll be fine."

Paul's plan worked. Fifteen minutes later we were riding in a Chevy Chevelle heading toward Akron, Ohio.

35

Jeff and Julie

Chevelles were always one of my favorite muscle cars. They had a sleek, sexy design. This was a 1970 SS coupe with a green exterior, skinny white pin striping down the hood and sides, white-walled Firestone tires, and a black interior. It was a sharp car and I was happy to be offered a ride, not to mention getting out of Willoughby Hills and away from Mama Lucia's less than welcoming clientele. As we were walking up to the Chevelle the blonde-haired twenty-something male driver stepped out with a big smile and bounded over to us, shaking Paul's hand and then mine.

"Morning, I'm Jeff, my girl Julie is in the passenger seat. You two can get in the back. Where you headin' to today?"

"Trying to get to I-70 if we can," said Paul.

"Oh, well I can't take you that far." said Jeff. "But I can maybe take you over to Ashland near I-71, how's that?"

"Great!" I said. "That'll really help us out, from there it's not too far to I-70 near Columbus."

We got into the car and introduced ourselves to Julie, who had her arms crossed and seemed a bit apprehensive about sharing the space with us.

"First we have to stop at our house in Wadsworth, a bit west of Akron, but don't worry, it's kind of on the way to Ashland, okay?"

"Not a problem," said Paul.

On the way to Jeff and Julie's he talked about his job at the Firestone plant on the production line.

"It's not the most exciting work, but the money and benefits, like a big discount on tires, are good," said Jeff. "You probably noticed the new tires on our Chevelle? The odor in the plant is the worst part, I can handle the hours and repetition of my job. But the continuous smell of rubber and other chemicals, that gets to me. Julie works at the local Kroger's supermarket in the bakery department. She likes to bring home the day old doughnuts to try and cheer me up."

Julie still didn't seem to be entirely comfortable with us being in their car. She spent more time staring out the front and side windows then looking at us, even after we told her about being college students trying to get to California, but Jeff was so gregarious and friendly I felt reasonably welcome. We made it to Jeff and Julie's house in less than forty-five minutes, and it was barely nine a.m. Their home, a Cape Cod, was small but looked well-maintained from the outside. The front porch overlooking the street looked like a great place to sit in the summertime, but they invited us into the living room.

"C'mon in," said Jeff. "We need to pick up a few things before heading to Ashland, you can use the bathroom if you want." Julie whispered something to Jeff which I couldn't make out, but I did hear Jeff say, "don't worry, they're cool, it won't be any problem, I promise."

We walked into a clean and neatly furnished living room. A large green couch with well-used sunken in cushions, coffee table, two end tables with Tiffany style lamps, a tan bean bag chair, a well-used blue La-Z-Boy chair with patches on the seat, a RCA record player with a collection of records on top of a makeshift table of cinder blocks and wood planks, and a small Zenith television filled the space.

"This is a nice place," I said.

"Thank you," said Julie. She seemed to be more relaxed and warming up to us. "The bathroom is down the hall if you need it, or have a seat on the couch."

I headed for the bathroom as Jeff walked upstairs, Julie went to the kitchen, and Paul sat in the La-Z-Boy. When I came out Jeff and Julie were sitting on the living room couch, a bong on the coffee table, along with four glasses of ice water and a plate with a dozen doughnuts. Julie had put on a record, "Freewheelin" by Bob Dylan, which was quietly playing in the background.

"Want to get high?" asked Jeff. It was a bit early in the morning for that, even for me, but I didn't want to seem rude, plus I thought it might make the day go smoother.

"Why not?" So I grabbed a chocolate covered donut, sat down on the bean bag chair and waited for Jeff to light the bong.

"This is pretty good weed," he said. "We bought it from a friend in Willoughby this morning, that's how we happened to see you two looking for a ride. It helps me get through the day at work and sometimes Julie and I feel the need for a mental health break and stay home. I couldn't make any more tires and Julie was tired of baking, so here we are. It gets tough being at work by four a.m. every day for her, and me, since I drive her there. Here you go, take a hit, Sean."

Needless to say Paul and I left Jeff and Julie's feeling a little better than when we had arrived. By 9:45 we were in the Chevelle and ready to roll. I made sure to grab a peanut covered doughnut before we left their living room. Even day old doughnuts tasted better than my gorp, especially after the bong. The world seemed a much nicer place and I had calmed down and was ready to head to Ashland and find our next ride. True to his word Jeff got us to the on-ramp to I-71 by 10:15 a.m.

"Thanks for the pot and doughnuts, it was a great start to the morning," I said.

"Not a problem, hope we made your day a bit better," said Jeff, as they headed back to Wadsworth.

Other than being higher than kites, the rest of the morning went smoothly, or maybe because we were so high it only seemed smooth. An Ohio state student took us to Columbus and I-70. Within twenty minutes a Wright State student picked us up and took us past Dayton and over to Greenfield, Indiana, where they left the Interstate and headed home to the small town of Maxwell. It was around two p.m. and the sun was blazing. I was sweaty and fanning myself with our 'WEST' sign. I ate a sleeve of graham crackers smeared with peanut butter out of sheer boredom. A ride didn't seem to be coming in the foreseeable future and my buzz had worn off.

Michael McCullough

Indy 500

Like life, there are decisions made when hitchhiking and almost entirely dependent on others that can change the day, relationships, or where you end up quite unexpectedly. My life had been blown off course over a year ago and was still drifting listlessly. We waited and waited for another ride next to the on-ramp near the rural town of Greenfield. They seemed to have an aversion for trees and instead corn, hay, and wheat fields dominated the landscape. Paul and I watched maybe ten cars in total ignore us as they drove up to I-70. The lack of vehicles didn't give either of us much hope of finding a ride anytime soon. I ate my peanut doughnut while pacing up and down the ramp and tried to learn to be patient, which was never one of my strengths.

Paul said, "C'mon Sean, let's take a chance and walk up to the Interstate, maybe someone will pull over before a cop comes along."

"I'm with you, better than standing here." It was a short walk up the ramp where we set our packs next to a speed limit sign. Our risky move paid off as less than ten minutes later a light blue 1973 Plymouth Barracuda slammed on its brakes, moved to the shoulder of the road as dust flew in the air from the squealing tires, and the passenger door suddenly flew open.

"Hey guys!" yelled a vivacious, red-haired, lovely looking thirty-something year old woman. She was holding onto the steering wheel and leaning across the front seat.

"I'm heading toward Indianapolis, care for a lift?" 'Whammer Jammer' by the J. Geils Band was blasting from her 8-track and I began dancing to the Cuda.

I didn't think twice, pushed up the front seat so Paul would have to get in the back, tossed him Atlas, and climbed in. "Hello, I'm Sean, that's Paul," I said with as much enthusiasm as possible. "Thanks for stopping. We were worried about being stuck out here, lots of farms and not many opportunities to get a ride. Man, this is a nice car."

"Yeah, love this car, it's my ex's, he had to give it up in our divorce which was finalized last Monday. Burned his butt to have to hand me the keys to his prize Cuda," she laughed. "Oh, I'm glad to offer help; it's nice to have company on my commute home from work. I'm Mary Ann, and I live in Homecroft, a bit south of Indianapolis, is that direction okay with you guys?"

Man she could talk, but maybe she was just a bit nervous from picking up two strange men and was keeping the conversation going in an attempt to cover that up.

"Absolutely," said Paul. "We're trying to get as far west as possible, stopping in Yellowstone and then out to the coast."

"Cool," she said. "But why hitchhike, why not just drive your own car?"

Paul seemed to be taking the bulk of the speaking for us and continued, "This seemed like a nice way to meet all sorts of people, see places we may not have checked out if we left the decisions all up to the two of us. What's your job?"

The Cuda hummed along on the Interstate, Mary Ann seemed to enjoy easily passing people, cruising from the far right lane to the middle and quickly to the left lane before relaxing a bit on the gas pedal and moving back to the middle. It wasn't herky-jerky, reckless driving, she was obviously in control and loved the power. The breeze from the windows was blowing her red hair around.

Mary Ann smiled and said, "I'm a dental technician in Knightstown, want me to check either of your mouths out for cavities? I don't have any Novocain at home, but plenty of vodka to numb any discomfort you might feel before the exam." She looked over at me and laughed.

"Not today, thanks, I think my teeth are in good shape, as a matter of fact I had a cleaning in January," Paul said.

"Excellent, glad are you taking care of your dental health, what about you, Sean?"

"Hmm, I think my last time at the dentist was last summer and no cavities for me. I wore braces for more than three years and went to the orthodontist all the time when I was in junior high, so that probably helped my teeth. It made me even more awkward around girls, but at least my teeth got straightened out. But if you want to make me a vodka drink and check out my mouth I'm good with that," I said, looking in her direction with my best smile. Probably not the most appropriate thing to say to a woman I just met and was nice enough to give us a ride, but Mary Ann chuckled at my answer. Changing the subject, I mentioned a flowery fragrance in the car that I had first become aware of after getting buckled up.

"Thanks for noticing, Sean, that's probably my perfume. Do you like it?" she asked.

"Absolutely, it's, a bit...lemony and... I don't know, I'm not good with scents, but it really smells nice."

"Charlie, that's what the perfume is called, my patients seem to like it, glad you do too," Mary Ann answered. "I still need to celebrate my divorce, Tuesday this week is my day off, a bit weird, but I have to work Saturday instead, why not come back to my apartment? I'll call my friend Vicky to come over, we can have pizza delivered and enjoy this warm summer night sitting on my deck drinking vodka tonics, or screwdrivers, or whatever suits your fancy, what do you say?" she asked, glancing in my direction.

Before I could get "Yes" out of my mouth, Paul surprisingly said, "We appreciate the invitation, but I think we'll pass." I looked back at him shooting daggers with my eyes. What the hell was he thinking? Here was a woman who seemed to be basically saying, "Spend the night with my friend and me" and the idiot says no? I couldn't wrap my head around this, especially with Paul's reputation as a hound dog, trying to pick up a different woman each night he was in a bar or at a party, and thought about telling Mary Ann, "hey if Paul doesn't want to come over, fine, but I sure do."

Instead, Mary Ann, a bit taken aback too, said, "oh, that's too bad, well the least I can do is drop you off on the other side of Indy, back near I-70, that'll help, right?"

"Yeah, great, that will be just great," I sarcastically said. Ten minutes later we were unceremoniously dropped off on the shoulder of I-70 at exit 59, a few miles west of where I could have spent the night with pizza, vodka, and two women. Damn.

Mary Ann said, "call me if you come through Indy again, okay?" and wrote down her phone number, which I took instead of entrusting the idiot Paul. The last time I saw her she was waving to us and driving off into the sunset back to Homecroft. We were left holding our packs, literally, with our thumbs stuck out, wondering who would come along next. This location was not anywhere I wanted to spend the night.

The Government Man

Paul was lucky, instead of me trying to punch him out for ruining the night, a white, impeccably clean, brand new looking, Chevy Impala with U.S. government plates pulled up within five minutes of Mary Ann dropping us off. The power window rolled down and the driver, who appeared to be in his forties and had hair like Richard Roundtree, leaned over and said in a baritone voice, "need a ride?"

"Absolutely, yes, thank you!" I replied and happily jumped in the front seat. The heck with Paul, he could suffer in the back until I wasn't irritated with him anymore.

It was always interesting looking at people who gave us rides and trying to figure them out. Sometimes I felt like Harriet the Spy or Nate the Great, child detectives in younger reader books who were always looking for clues to be able to solve mysteries. This man was professional looking, well-groomed, black dress pants, polished shoes, and a light blue short sleeved dress shirt without a wrinkle or crease anywhere on it. The floor of the Impala was clean, no fast food bags, leaves, mud, or stones anywhere to be found. The light brown seats and upholstery seemed to not have any stains on them and even the dashboard and windows were spotless.

"That's an interesting tattoo on your forearm, does it have any meaning?" I asked.

"Thanks, it's two crossed cannons, it means I served in the Navy," the driver said.

"Don't you ever eat, smoke, or drink in here?" I asked. No doubt another rude question to start our ride with.

"I like to keep the car clean, besides, the agency I work for pays for it, so why not?" the man said.

"I noticed the government plates, what agency do you work for?" I asked.

"Very observant, now that doesn't really matter, does it?" he mysteriously replied. "Does that make you nervous?"

"No, not really," I said. "CIA, FBI, some secret Navy thing, it's all good, I'm okay not knowing. I've been a bit rude, that's Paul in the back, I'm Sean, and we're on our way to Yellowstone and then the California coast. We appreciate the ride, absolutely, thanks for picking us up."

"It's not a problem, I needed some company to help stay awake, it's getting a bit late and I've been driving a long time, over ten hours from Washington, D.C. and still about five hours to go. I can get you as far as Kansas City, how is that?" he asked.

"Excellent, great," I said, unfolding my road map and taking a look at the distance. "But isn't it usually a six plus hour drive from here, going through St. Louis and then over to KC?"

"Not when you work for my agency and drive a government car with these plates, the speed limit doesn't matter that much to me," he said.

I checked the odometer and he was maintaining seventy-five miles per hour in the fifty-five mph speed zone. We were going to get to Kansas City fast, probably near ten p.m., actually earlier since we passed into the central time zone once crossing into Illinois. I had to adjust my Timex watch, no sense being an hour off.

"What do you guys do when not hitchhiking around the country?"

Paul seemed to finally recover from his own shock at turning down Mary Ann's invitation and began to carry the conversation. "I'm a geology major and football player in college in Upstate NY, Sean is going for an earth science and English double major at the same college. I think Sean is going to end up writing books or magazine articles on science subjects, right Sean?" Paul didn't wait for an answer before continuing. "It's probably a bit weird, but I've been trying to collect rocks, minerals, and take photographs of geological features as we've been passing through states."

"That doesn't sound weird at all."

Paul went on, "so right now this area of Missouri is mainly sedimentary rocks, like shale, limestone and sandstone. There have been a few sea levels rising and falling over millions of years depositing rock. There could also be types of volcanic rock from the Proterozoic Eon deep underneath the sedimentary layers. Let's see, what else can I remember? Oh, yeah, glaciers also helped form features in Missouri. Actually galena is the official state mineral, it's used to make lead."

Paul seemed to want to go on, I think he was in some kind of special geology zone in his head and wanted to spew it all out, but the Gov't Man had had enough.

"Well, that's all pretty interesting Paul," said the Gov't Man. "Thanks for the quick geology lesson."

Our only stop was for gas and then to buy food from McDonald's, which we scarfed down before getting back in the Impala. The Gov't Man wasn't going to have any stinky fast food bags in his car. We flew through St. Louis and continued toward Kansas City.

Mystery Gov't Man, we never did learn his name, stuck true to his word and let us off at the exit to Blue Springs, Missouri, a little bit east of Kansas City. He was the first person we met that didn't want to disclose their exact exit or place they may really be heading to. Smart thinking, to be a bit cautious, these drivers were taking a risk by picking up two hitchhikers. Paul and I weren't sure what steps to take now. It was dark, the odds of anyone stopping were slim, we really didn't know where we were, except on I-70 outside of Kansas City, and we were tired.

"Let's sleep down there on the grass, Sean," said Paul.

"Down there, on that slope, twenty feet from the highway?" I asked incredulously.

"You have a better idea?" he said. I had to admit I didn't, other than finding a motel. Not seeing one within walking distance I reluctantly agreed to go down the slope. We waited until the headlights passed from a bunch of cars and climbed over the guardrail. It was a bit noisy, but we were hidden from the traffic. After taking a whiz, I put my boots next to Atlas, stuffed my socks into the dirty clothes bag, unrolled my mat and sleeping bag, and climbed in. I found KMBZ on my transistor radio and listened to a few songs, including the Eagles, "Take it Easy" before falling into a restless sleep.

47

Michael McCullough

Rocks, Guns, & Barbeque

Anticipation
Boredom, fumes, dirt, horns, hunger
Put trust in strangers

A brilliant sunrise greeted us in the morning. I felt like the bags under my eyes had bags of their own, I was nineteen going on sixty-five. Changing my clothes on a grassy slope off of this busy highway with commuters speeding past was not easy. I propped our packs up and crouched behind them to pee, put on new underwear and sprayed on some deodorant. I wore my earth science club shirt, socks, sneakers, cutoff shorts, and brushed my hair and teeth. I felt like a homeless guy or hobo, and really, probably was. If it was the 1930's I probably would have tried to ride the rails. Paul changed into shorts meant for a geologic dig, pockets galore. He put on his geology club shirt, socks, and sneakers. We both hooked our hiking boots to our backpacks. I'm surprised he didn't hook his rock pick to the shorts. We did our fifty morning push-ups and sit-ups on the hill, then ate a gourmet meal of rye bread with peanut butter washed down with water from our canteens. Paul, Mr. Fruit Man, had two bananas and gave me one of his apples which I ate on the way up the slope to the Interstate. It was my turn to stand with my thumb out and the "WEST" sign propped against Atlas, while Paul leaned against the guardrail and read his *Rocks and Minerals* paperback book.

"Let's make a bet," I said to Paul. "How many times today do we get thrown the bird? I'm going with four. Plus, how many times will a car or truck swerve at us pretending like they're going to hit us, I'll go with three. What do you think?"

"I'll take five birds and two swerves," answered Paul. "What's the winner get?"

"Loser buys the winner two beers next time we are in a bar."

"Perfect," said Paul. "I'm thirsty already."

Time passed slowly as cars zipped by. It was morning; people were in a hurry to get somewhere most of them didn't really want to be... work. Who was going to stop on a busy highway, take a chance on the two guys standing there and maybe be late for their job?

"Ah, there's one bird, I hope you're keeping track," I said. To pass time I began reading a chapter from *The Elements of Style* on writing paragraphs.

Three hours later... three hours during which I sucked in fumes like my mouth was wrapped around a semi-truck exhaust stack...three hours that seemed more like three days, a dull red 1970 Chevrolet pickup truck with a white top slowed down and pulled over about fifty feet from us. It took a few seconds to wonder if he was one of those people teasing us with a ride or really meant for us to run up to the truck. The driver was wearing a cowboy hat and waved at us through the rear window as if to say, "C'mon, hurry up and get in!" I got to the door first while Paul fussed putting his book back in his pack. The window was rolled down and the guy said, "put your packs in the back, boys, and let's get on the road before someone hits us."

We placed our packs in the bed of the truck, I sat in the middle next to the cowboy and Paul was by the door. The Chevy was a manual shift on the steering column, a reliable ride, even if a bit rough on the road. "Where are you boys headed?" asked the cowboy.

"As far west as we can go," I said. "First Yellowstone and then out to the coast."

"Whoa, boy, that's a long trip. I can get you to Topeka, then you'll have to find other rides. Oh yeah, you can call me Tom, what'll y'all be named?" said the cowboy.

"I'm Sean, he's Paul, we're from Western New York," I answered. "He's a geology major and I'm still deciding, English, science who knows. I'm wondering why you have that pistol next to you?"

"Make you worried?" asked Tom. "It's legal in Kansas to carry a weapon as long as it's not concealed. Besides, I'm a Kansas City cop, just got off the night shift and a couple of hours of overtime."

"Oh, well that's a relief. How long a drive is it to Topeka?" Paul asked.

"It's pretty quick, maybe eighty minutes. Before I leave you there, though, it'll be close to lunchtime so we can stop at Gates Barbeque, guarantee you'll like their pulled pork sandwiches. I bet you haven't had a decent meal in a while, so this will give you a chance to fill up before waiting for another ride. It's right off the highway, there should be no problem getting another lift," said Tom.

"That sounds awesome," agreed Paul. "I'm starved for some real food. Our breakfast was peanut butter on rye bread."

"I assure you this barbeque place will have better offerings," said Tom.

A little more than an hour later we came up to the exit for the restaurant and pulled into the parking lot. Hickory wood smoke permeated the air from the cookers in the rear of the building. Cop Tom left us on our own, ordered his usual food for takeout, waved, and drove off. Paul and I decided to order and eat at one of the picnic tables out front instead of heading right back to the highway. Two pulled pork sandwiches with coleslaw on top, two orders of baked beans, two chocolate chip cookies the size of a small pie and two sixteen ounce Cokes later, we were stuffed. It was hard to get up and walk the mile or so to the Interstate, but we did it, there wasn't much of a choice at this point.

It was mid-afternoon and the Kansas sun was beating on us. I rubbed Coppertone on my arms, neck, and legs. Paul and I took turns standing with our "WEST" sign while the other one sat on the stony shoulder of the road or leaned on the guardrail. It was a pretty busy on-ramp but no one seemed interested in giving us a ride. To pass time we had a contest throwing stones at the road signs near us. My arm wasn't built for throwing so I lost every time. I wasn't giving up on the free beer though so I kept counting birds thrown and cars trying to hit us. At eight p.m. it was three birds and two swervers, so I was winning on the birds being thrown, but running out of time, I hoped, for cars swerving to hit us. I really didn't like cars swerving toward us and didn't care if I lost that part of the bet. By nine p.m. we were extremely discouraged and wondering if this was our spot for the night. This was an insanely long time to wait for any kind of ride while we were next to a busy Interstate on-ramp. Apparently people in Kansas weren't excited about giving a ride to a couple of long-haired guys carrying backpacks.

Michael McCullough

Uncle Sam Wants You!

Paul and I were ready to find a spot in the fields and bed down for another night under the stars when a gold four-door 1969 Ford Galaxy came to a sudden stop right in front of us. We looked at each other and Paul said, "What the hell, this could be great or one of our worst lifts ever." As I nodded my head in agreement a man opened the front passenger side door, staggered a bit while taking a step, and had to hold onto the door so he didn't fall. He was wearing army fatigues, black boots, and an army trucker's cap. He wobbled over a few feet and began to pee on the guardrail.

"Hey, hey, you guys look like you need a lift, climb into the back seat," he slurred while turning around and zipping up his pants. I hesitantly opened the rear door and moved over to the far side with Atlas. Paul slid in next to me with his pack. Uncharacteristically we both put on our seatbelts. There were several beer cans on the floor of the car and a small cooler on the front seat between the driver and passenger.

"Hellllooo," said the driver, also dressed in fatigues. "They call me Jack and that man trying to get back in is Gary. We've had a few beers tonight, so Gary is a bit wobbly, but don't you worry, I'm good to go. If those empties bother you, kick 'em under the seat."

A car came up from behind and blared its horn. Gary threw them the bird and closed the door as Jack pressed the gas pedal. "Where you guys heading off to?" asked Gary.

"On our way west, hopefully making the coast," I replied. "How far are you two going tonight," I asked.

"We have to be back on base at Ft. Riley by two a.m., so not that far, guess we can drop you off near Abilene, then circle back to base, that's about eighty minutes from here, you okay with that Gary?" asked Jack. Gary was slugging down another Old Milwaukee and mumbled, "kay with me."

I was still nervous about Jack's driving but he was staying near the speed limit and kept the car between the lines, even when sipping the beer between his legs.

"Never asked what your names are," said Jack.

"Paul and Sean," replied Paul. He continued even though not asked, "Yeah, I'm a geology major and Sean thinks he's going to write the next great American novel."

"Hah, make sure you include us in your book then, Sean. Two brave Army privates who drive deuce and a half's or any other truck they order us to."

"Do you carry a cooler of Old Milwaukee's with you then?" I joked.

"Not quite," laughed Gary, "just cigs to help pass the time. Want one now?" Gary lit a Marlboro and I unrolled my window. I could take second-hand smoke in bars, but in a car it seemed to give me motion sickness.

"No thanks," said Paul. "I'm in training for football and Sean here is a bit of a health nut, except for when it comes to alcohol."

"You should have said so, here, a beer for each of you," said Jack, passing us a can. We finished our beers as Jack pulled into a rest stop outside of Abilene.

"This is the end of the line for us, Sean and Paul. Time to grab your gear and find another ride," said Jack. "I think Gary and I will go inside and piss before heading back to camp. The last thing we need is to be reported AWOL."

"Thanks for the ride and beer," I said. "We thought we'd be stuck in Topeka, so it's nice to make it further down the road."

A few minutes later Gary and Jack drove off in their Galaxy, giving us a salute as they entered the Interstate. We saw them driving in the other direction toward the Army base and hoped they made it back safely and on time.

It was 11:30 p.m., pretty late, but Paul and I decided to walk up the on-ramp and out onto the interstate hoping for a driver that might take us along for a night ride. Instead, a Kansas highway patrol car pulled up in front of us with his lights flashing.

"What are you boys doing out here tonight?" the officer gruffly asked as he got out of his car, tightening his belt as he was walking toward us. He was probably five feet eight and built like a fullback, powerful looking, like a whiskey barrel with arms and legs.

"Hello, sir," said Paul. "We're trying to catch a ride out of here; we're headed toward the Denver area."

"You know it's illegal for a pedestrian to be on the Interstate, right, why didn't you read the sign that's right back there?"

"I did see it, sir, but we didn't want to get caught having to stay overnight at this rest area and were hoping it would be easier to get a ride out here closer to the road," I said, noticing the officer's badge and his name, Quinn.

"Hand over your identification, driver's license, passport, whatever you have, I need to check them," said the officer. Looking over our driver's licenses, he was impressed by the distance we had traveled. "New York, huh, you two have come a long way."

"Yes, Officer Quinn, we've done pretty well getting to Kansas in only a few days and met some interesting people along the way," I said.

"Quinn, correct, you are observant, Harlan Quinn. Now I don't care where you wait for a ride, hang from the light pole, wait at the restroom, stand in the parking lot or close to the entrance of the on-ramp, but you are not waiting on my Interstate, understand? I have to give you each a ticket for trespassing. When I come by here again I strongly suggest you not be on the road, understand? If you are, it will be a night in jail, okay?"

We both nodded in agreement as we took the tickets and said, "yes sir, no problem, we won't be on the road again." With that Officer Harlan Quinn disappeared into the night.

Riders on the Storm

After our encounter with Officer Harlan Quinn, Paul and I trudged back toward the rest area. We had given up on getting a ride this night and wandered the grounds wondering what to do. We didn't dare pitch the tent which would have made it easier for Officer Quinn to see us still near the Interstate, and we were pretty sure neither he nor passersby would appreciate us camping out there. Getting another ticket for trespassing on an Interstate, or worse, taken to jail as a transient, didn't appeal to either one of us. I could picture myself calling home and telling Mom, "Hey, I'm doing okay, just this issue with being in jail in Abilene, Kansas and needing some bail money." I'm not sure her or Dad would have appreciated that. Actually I am sure Dad would have told the cops to leave me there for a couple of days so I could learn some kind of stupid lesson. He was always about me learning a lesson.

There were a few tall Bur Oak trees near the rear fence line of the rest area, so we simply unrolled our mats and laid out our bags. I grabbed a bag of gorp from Atlas and a canteen for a late night snack. After eating Paul and I took turns washing up in the rest area facilities. It was a warm, cloudy night with the not so sweet odor of freshly laid manure in the air from the surrounding farms. I could hear cars and semis continually cruising by on the Interstate. Often headlights would shine from the parking lot over through the trees toward us as people pulled in to use the facilities or needed a short break from the highway. My little transistor radio wouldn't pick up any stations out here in the boonies, so I had to be content with the sound of nighthawks permeating the sky.

Many times I would feel exhausted and know I had to go to sleep, then, after getting into bed, or in my sleeping bag, my brain would begin remembering things from the past better left hidden, and coming up with a dozen different things I should have done or said instead of what really transpired. This night, assisted by the birds, trucks, pungent manure, headlights, and wondering what tomorrow would bring, was made for insomnia. I began to flashback to a night at the BVI (Brockport Village Inn). There were so many bars in the small college town of Brockport, each having their usual clientele. Specials on drinks during the week or people wanting to let loose on weekends, however, would bring in crowds of students who weren't normal partiers searching for a good time. It wasn't unusual for Paul and other buddies of mine to stop in at different bars, cruising Main Street, having a drink or two at each place and trying to discover where we thought the hottest girls would be hanging out, even though the Barge Inn was our normal go-to place.

The BVI was known for the "Mug Club". Students could buy a glass mug at the beginning of the semester, only fifty were allowed. When you came in and asked for your mug by name for just a dollar you would get a sixteen ounce Bloody Mary or beer. I never had my own mug, the BVI was not a typical stop on my nights out, I always thought of it as kind of a dive, but Paul and several football players had mugs. Paul would go in with me, tell me the name of a teammate to say, and voila, I'd have a mug for the night, hoping the entire time the real player didn't show up. The bartender would stare at me, not knowing to believe if I was really the player, but then ultimately deciding what difference did it make? Money was money. The jukebox was playing Bad Company, "Feel Like Makin' Love". It was Saturday night in late March near the middle of the spring semester, 1976, and the bar was packed. I began with a Boilermaker to start things off. The first one went down quickly and I made Paul buy the second round.

As Paul made his way to the bar a former girlfriend, Amy, came near me and said, "I'm surprised to see you here Sean."

Her curly shoulder-length brown hair cascaded down around her beautiful face and hazel eyes. My heart skipped a beat whenever I saw or thought of her, but the ending of the relationship was so traumatic I didn't have the capacity to deal with it appropriately. I wasn't sure what to say, and could only come up with, "Well, it definitely wasn't to find you!" and I grabbed the shot glass Paul was handing me, downed the whiskey and finished half of my second beer in a few seconds. It really wasn't what I wanted to say; maybe the alcohol was having a bad effect on me that night. Instead of becoming more outgoing and friendly, seeing Amy flipped my switch the other way.

She just said, "I'm sorry to hear that," turned around and went to the back room of the bar. I finished the beer watching her go from my life again. I put a quarter in the jukebox and selected, "Right Place Wrong Time" by Dr. John, quite appropriate for this time of the night.

Paul said, "You're an idiot, Sean, go after her."

"I did that with her a couple of times, made a jackass of myself and was blown-off; she wouldn't even tell me why all of a sudden she hated me, how much rejection should I take?" I asked. "You keep telling me there are a lot of women out there, variety is the key."

"Yeah, well, I thought she was special to you?"

"Who knows anymore?" I was getting pissed off. "I haven't seemed too special to her for quite a while, right? Just leave me the fuck alone, okay?"

I quickly finished my second beer, and headed back to the bar pushing a couple of guys aside so I could get our third round. This was going to be quite a night.

"Hey shithead," one of them said. "You spilled my beer you bastard."

"Fuck you," was my witty reply. I picked up my next shot and downed it and then grabbed my mug just as his friend pushed my shoulder from behind, spilling some of the beer on my pants and the floor, which totally pissed me off. What a waste of good beer. Paul had been watching the scene unfold and as I turned around to confront the jackass and was considering throwing the rest of my beer in his face, he put both hands on the guy's shoulders and tossed him back into a nearby table. At the same time the guy's friend shoved me and as I was turning toward him, deftly holding onto what remained of my beer in my left hand, I brought my right arm back to throw a punch at his head, using the boxing skills Jason had taught me. Instead a bouncer grabbed my arm and none too gently led me to the exit door and out the steps, grabbing my beer mug at the same time. Paul, being followed by a second bouncer, was right behind me. The two idiots were able to stay in the bar, which seemed unfair.

"Now what?" said Paul. "Was it really necessary for you to piss off those guys? The drinks were going down so easy. Let's get out of here, you can buy me a beer at the Barge Inn for the trouble you started."

"Hey, it wasn't my fault; they started it, not me."

"You're the imbecile that pushed your way to the bar, spilling that guy's drink. Oh, crap, now what?" said Paul, as two of Brockport's finest came walking up the alley way toward us. Evidently the bartender or the bouncers had made a quick phone call.

"Turn around son, I need to cuff you," said the taller of the two cops. Son? What did that mean, son? He was old though, probably in his forties, with a bit of a pot belly hanging over his pants, so maybe I looked really young to him. Maybe the cop was trying to appear friendly. It seemed like keeping my mouth shut might be a good plan, especially after the whiskey shots and beers. The other, skinnier cop, with a mustache similar to Burt Reynolds, handcuffed Paul.

"What did we do, we didn't do anything wrong, do you really need to cuff us?" I asked.

"That's not what we heard from the owner of the bar. We're going to take you in for drunk and disorderly conduct in a public place."

Paul said, "But it was self-defense, those two came after Sean and I was only trying to help out."

I was a bit tipsy, a bit high on adrenaline, a bit sad from seeing Amy again and not being able to speak to her honestly, or her to me, and told the cops, "I wasn't drunk and disorderly in public, I was drunk and disorderly in the bar, and it's their fault I'm out here! Besides, I was only dancing to the music and maybe I accidentally bumped one of those guys, they're the ones who began harassing us, they should be getting charged."

"That's not the way we heard it. Let's go."

And that's how I got my first ride in a police car while wearing handcuffs. An hour later Paul and I had misdemeanor tickets for D and D, which would involve a court visit at a date to be determined, in front of Amy's Dad, who happened to be the Town Justice. I had a feeling that night in court wasn't going to be a good one. The cops said we were lucky to not get another ticket for assault. It was only after they had checked with other people in the bar that the additional charge wasn't given. There were fights every weekend in town, so this was nothing new to the police.

The last thing I needed was a Driving While Intoxicated, so we left my Mom's car I had borrowed for the night parked on Main Street. It wasn't even midnight yet so Paul and I walked to our second home, the Barge Inn, where hopefully life would be a bit more peaceful.

With those thoughts finally drifting from my brain I fell asleep under the Oak tree, thinking it was Amy I should have chased in the bar instead of trying to start a fight with two random strangers. Sometimes I was so stupid.

***

Evil takes all shapes
shows up unexpectedly
resist or submit

The morning finally arrived and a brilliant sun-filled Kansas sky greeted Paul and I as we crawled out of our sleeping bags. We took turns going to the rest area bathroom to get shaved and as clean as possible considering our circumstances. I put on my cutoffs, clean socks, boots, and 'keep on truckin' shirt. Paul wore his cutoffs, boots, and a plaid short sleeve shirt. He made us do our requisite fifty push-ups and sit-ups in the grassy area. I was still mad from some of my thoughts during last night's flashback and added in six hard wind sprints between light posts, made a bit tougher with boots on instead of sneakers. Our breakfast was another peanut butter on rye bread sandwich and water as we walked up the on-ramp toward the Interstate, taking care not to go onto the highway itself. Paul took the first shift standing while holding our "WEST" sign and I sat on the shoulder of the road reading about Sal Paradise longing for the freedom of the road in *On the Road* by Jack Kerouac. Thankfully, within an hour, a tan Volkswagen bus with a white top that we had seen pull into the rest area for a few minutes stopped; the front seat passenger offered us a ride as the side door slid open and the Iron

Butterfly song, "In-A-Gadda-Da-Vida" came blasting out of the speakers. I hated Iron Butterfly.

Paul said, "let's get in," and tossed his backpack on the van floor. I was hesitant, but the alternative of standing on the ramp of this rest area in Abilene, Kansas any longer didn't appeal to me. The only seats were for the driver and front passenger. A man and woman sat on the puke-green colored shag carpeted floor behind them, another woman, her head bobbing up and down and side to side, sat at the back of the van on a small bean bag chair. Her movements weren't even in sync with the music piercing my skull. I immediately had a bad feeling about this ride, but wanted to get away from the possibility of seeing any more Kansas police officers. So I placed Atlas on the floor near me, sat down and said, "Okay" as the scraggly bearded driver turned down the music and asked, "where are you two heading?"

Paul said, "Eventually California, but for now as close to Denver as we can get."

"Hey, we're headed to Denver too," said the driver. "Shut the door and settle in for a ride." With that he pressed the accelerator and we began moving slowly down the highway.

With muscle laden, college football playing, former high school wrestler, barroom brawler Paul by my side, I figured we could handle most situations, including this ride.

"I'm George," said the driver. "And that's Lenny, with a y" pointing to the right.

"Of Mice and Men", I mumbled to Paul, but he didn't seem to hear me.

"Everyone introduce yourselves," said George, as Lenny kept staring at us.

"I'm Roger, this is my girlfriend Rita, keep your hands off her, don't stare at her, don't ask her a question unless I tell you it's okay, she's mine," he croaked. Rita, for her part, looked sadly around the van and at us, before lowering her head and continuing to paint her toenails a deep shade of red.

"In the back sitting on the bean bag, that's Penny," stated George. "Don't mind her; she's a bit high from her morning breakfast of LSD."

Indeed, Penny didn't seem to have much of an idea or care that Paul and I were in the van, I'm not sure she knew she was in a van riding somewhere.

"You two want a tab?" asked Lenny. I could drink more alcohol than most and stay standing, got high from pot at least twice a week, and been offered LSD in the past, but my self-awareness was keen enough to know that it was not a drug for me. My brain was already filled with a wild imagination and if I went tripping somewhere who knew if I was ever going to come back?

"No, thanks," I replied, shaking my head.

"None for me," said Paul. "I need to stay in shape for football in the fall and can't take any drugs." Which was true, but then again, he was the only person I knew who could out-party me on booze, football season or not.

As we continued driving down the highway, Rita had finished painting her toenails and now was working on her fingernails. This time she used different colors while painting stripes on each nail, which was kind of interesting to watch. Rita seemed to be a perfectionist when it came to applying the polish.

George asked, "Hey, what do you two do for money out here on the road?" My guard immediately went up.

"We have a few dollars between us, otherwise we'll stop for a couple of days and work for a farmer or find temporary work elsewhere," I lied and winked at Paul. "We might get a dry barn to sleep in, a meal or two, and earn a couple of bucks to keep us going."

Lenny with a 'y' was staring at me and suddenly pulled out a knife that he used to pick his teeth with.

George said, "We've found it pretty easy to walk into churches along the way and grab money from donation boxes or collection baskets. They seem to be trusting of strangers and it's a convenient method for us to keep gas in the van and food in our stomachs. One or two of us will start talking to the pastor or staff and the others will grab the money. We always leave a little in the baskets so it doesn't look obvious that we took anything. Besides, aren't churches supposed to be helping poor people like us?"

I was a bit shocked and it probably showed on my face. Stealing, especially from churches, wow, that was taking things to a whole different level. I didn't have to be baptized and confirmed into the Presbyterian Church to know that.

"Hey, don't worry," said George. "We won't try and make you steal anything. It's just with us giving you a ride and all, well, we all have to pitch in to make it work, don't you see?"

"Actually," said Lenny with a 'y', "we're going to stop at this gas station coming up in Hays, fill-up and grab some food. You and Paul here can pay for it so we can keep moving toward Denver."

Rita was finishing up her fingernails, Roger was staring at us, George kept peering in the rear view mirror at us, and Penny, well, she was still off in la-la land. There was no help to be had by anyone in this van.

"Sure," agreed Paul. "You pull the van up to the store and Sean and I will see what cash we can come up with."

A few minutes later we left the Interstate and stopped at the Conoco gas station. A horn from a vehicle parked nearby was stuck and filled the air with an obnoxious sound. It was blistering hot, at least eighty-five degrees, and bugs were swarming in the parking lot. My senses were overwhelmed. Before the VW was fully stopped I opened the side door, grabbed Atlas, and took off, not even slowing down or looking back to see if Paul was following. There wasn't a chance I was staying in that van or near those people any longer. Paul could make his own decision. I made it to the road before hearing Paul, "hold up Sean," he yelled, and turned around to see him running in my direction.

Once Paul caught up to me we kept walking down the road toward the on-ramp, neither of us looking behind, not sure what was going to happen if the VW caught up with us.

"I wasn't going to stay in that van either; you had to give me a minute to get out."

"They were disgusting, insane people!" I said. "I couldn't stay near them for another second. I figured it was your business if you wanted to continue riding with them!"

A Savior

Sometimes miracles do happen. A sage green two-door 1973 Plymouth Valiant with Kansas plates pulled up alongside us before we got to the on-ramp. A late twenty or early thirty something year old woman with shoulder length Farrah Fawcett style light-brown hair, an angelic face and sunglasses on, said, "I saw you two in the parking lot and yelled to see if you wanted a ride, but I guess you were running too fast to hear me, or maybe that car horn was too loud? I'm heading to the Denver area and could use some company if you want to hop in?"

"Absolutely," I said, and grabbed the front seat, immediately noticing the evocative odor of musk from her perfume and freckles on her arms and a few on her face. She was cute and I wanted to get out of Hays and away from the VW van and its occupants as fast as possible. Paul climbed in the back seat with our backpacks. I couldn't believe our luck as we went from riding with the devil and his helpers to an angel from heaven in a manner of minutes.

"Where are you heading?" she asked.

"As close to Windsor, Colorado as you can get us," I replied.

"Why the rush to get out of the VW?" she asked.

"They weren't exactly the friendliest of people and told us about their liking for robbing churches," I said.

"Eww, that sounds horrible! Now I see your hurry to find a new ride, I'm glad I can help out," she said. "You're in luck, I need to get to the Denver area as soon as possible due to a family emergency, so buckle up, watch for cops on the road and planes that fly along the Interstate checking speeds. Oh, and my name is Bonnie, what are yours?"

"I'm Sean, in the backseat is Paul, we're students at Brockport State in New York, traveling around the country for fun for a while," I said. Just a few minutes in Bonnie's car and I was already so much more relaxed, this was such a nicer atmosphere than the VW. I had the gift, or curse, of reading a room or people in almost any situation and feeling that they weren't being totally honest or comfortable sharing what really was going on in their head. My sense of empathy sometimes was overpowering and I had the habit of absorbing the feelings of others, which could leave me either happy or sad. Bonnie was pleasant, non-threatening, and welcoming, but I felt there was more to her story. Who knew if she was going to share it?

Even with that sense it was so different between riding with Bonnie and feeling trapped in the VW. I instantly felt at ease, and, as usual when a woman was beautiful and also confident enough to pick us up, attracted to her. We took off down the interstate, speed limit fifty-five miles per hour, at seventy-eighty mph. This was going to be a fast trip if we didn't get pulled over.

"Sean, there are some 8-track tapes in the glove box, pick one out and put it in the player so we can pass time faster," Bonnie said. Fleetwood Mac was the tape I selected, Paul and I had gone to their concert in Rochester during the winter. Like ten thousand other guys we both had a crush on Stevie Nicks. Unfortunately I had no idea where on the dashboard the tape player was located. Stupidly I tried two places, with Paul cracking up in the backseat, before Bonnie had to point to the actual player. So much for making a good impression on her, I thought to myself.

"Keep looking for planes, Sean," Bonnie said. So I kept an eye out through the front and side windows, not sure if she was playing a game seeing how gullible I was, or really was concerned with planes overhead checking our speed. It turned out I was in charge of the music, so when Fleetwood Mac finished I chose Elton John and then Sly and the Family Stone. Trying to pass time as we continued driving I began to ask Bonnie some questions:

"Where did you leave from today?"

"Oh, I live in the Wichita area. I'm a paralegal in a local law firm."

"Did you grow up near Denver?" She looked at me sideways, like not really wanting to answer. "Sorry, I don't mean to pry."

"It's okay, yeah, I went to high school in Englewood, just outside of Denver, and then college at Wichita State, which is how I ended up in a law firm there. Most of my family still lives in Englewood, so I go there quite a bit to visit, of course. But this trip is special; my Mom was just diagnosed with thyroid cancer, so I'm going there to be with her while she undergoes radiation treatment."

"Oh, I'm so sorry; I didn't mean to be so nosy. I'm sure your parents will love having you at home for however long you can be there."

"Yeah, I think so. Mom has always been my biggest supporter. Enough of that, I know where most of the speed traps are on I-70, but still need you to look for police planes, Sean, so keep glancing at the skies. Tell me, why did you two decide to hitchhike?"

Paul was sitting in the back mouthing the lyrics to "Honey Cat" and "Bennie and the Jets", so I answered.

"When we're standing on the shoulder of the road under a blazing hot sun or driving rainstorm I wonder the same thing. I guess we decided it would be more of an adventure if we took a risk with rides, meeting new people, and maybe going on roads or to towns we might not have if we drove ourselves."

"That kind of makes sense, I guess. Nothing I ever tried or would want to, but good for you two. I hope it all works out."

"Me too, thanks, I'm still trying to decide if it was the right decision, especially after that last ride."

It was around 300 miles to Bennett, Colorado. Bonnie made it there in a bit over four hours, pretty amazing with a fifty-five mph speed limit. Understandably, she had no desire to take us all the way to Windsor, as she really had to continue to Denver. I couldn't thank her enough for saving us from the VW and the quick ride. We stopped at a Texaco station and when Bonnie went inside to use the restroom, Paul paid for and filled her gas tank. It was the least we could do after she saved us from the evil van. I went to the pay phone and called Mr. Miller, an old friend and co-worker of my father's at Kodak in Rochester. He went on to become director of security at the Kodak Windsor plant.

Sometimes it's hard to tell what burdens people carry in their lives. Some like to talk about them as a kind of therapy session, others just keep their feelings bottled up inside. I could definitely appreciate both of those choices. We said our goodbyes to Bonnie as she took off as fast as possible on her journey to Englewood and waited for the Millers to come down and pick us up, despite my protests saying we could get a ride closer to their home.

Miller's Retreat

Rocky Mountain high
Colorado oasis
Home away from home

Mr. Miller seemed overjoyed as he sprang out of his car like a teenager when he came to pick up Paul and myself. I had known the Millers (Joe and Jean) since I was seven years old. Besides working with my father for many years in security at Kodak Park, they were in a flying club together. Mr. Miller had been a pilot in WWII, flying B-17 bombers over Europe. He continued his love of flying many years later by joining a club of six people, including my Dad, who shared costs of maintaining the plane and hangar fees for a four-seat Piper Cherokee. Despite my penchant for airsickness I loved going on flights around the Finger Lakes area with my family and the Millers. I had even earned my student pilot license at the age of sixteen, before I had a license to drive a car. For better or worse I stopped flying to concentrate on sports.

We went to the Miller's home in Rochester several times over a few years, where the plastic dome covered in-ground pool was a unique sight in the neighborhood of Rochester they lived in. Mr. Miller loved to swim and believed it was money well-spent with the winter weather we endured in Upstate New York.

We were riding along state highways and small town roads, a much calmer drive than on the Interstates and quite a welcome change. The Miller's 1975 maroon colored Pontiac Bonneville sailed along like the small planes we flew years ago did on calm days. The Rocky Mountains to the west were a stunning transition coming from the plains of the Midwest. Mr. Miller had transferred to the Windsor, Colorado Kodak plant a few months after my father turned down the job as head of security, and had been living here for nine years. It was always interesting pondering how different my life would have been if we had moved to Colorado.

I never saw Mr. Miller without a smile on his face, always quick to laugh, and at least one new bad joke to tell. He was the opposite of Mrs. Miller, who seemed to be reserved and never quite comfortable around children, teenagers, or now, hitchhikers. Considering our clothes and bodies that needed to be washed, I could understand some of her hesitancy of instantly welcoming us into their car and home.

"We already called your parents, Sean, so they know you made it this far and are safe with us," said Mr. Miller. "We didn't know your home phone number Paul, but you are welcome to use our phone to call your parents anytime you are with us."

"Thank you," we said in unison.

"It's only about an hour to our house, maybe then you two would like a quick swim to relax from the travels?" Mrs. Miller shot her husband a questioning look, like "why would you make such an offer?"

Her husband didn't seem to notice or care. "After that you can shower, use the washer to clean your clothes, and I'll grill a few steaks, okay?"

"That sounds fantastic," I said. "If there's anything we can do to help with dinner or around the house, let Paul or I know."

We pulled up to a beautiful, large, red tiled roofed, brick exterior ranch home on a small hill overlooking the town, and in the distance, a view of the foothills of the Rockies. An extension of the home housed their in-ground pool. Their yard, along with neighbors who lived further down the hill, was all small white stone instead of grass. This area around Windsor was considered semi-arid and the Millers needed a special permit to have a pool, even if it was indoors. This stop on the trip was going to be luxury living for us.

Within thirty minutes of arriving, Paul, Mr. Miller, and I were swimming. We only had our cutoff jeans to wear, which, with the look on her face, seemed to disgust Mrs. Miller even more; maybe because of the dirt ground into them or our bodies. The room with the pool was breathtaking, wall-to-wall windows with views of the mountains; it was a place I could stay in for weeks. Even though I wasn't much of a swimmer, being near water; whether a pool, river, lake, or ocean, always relaxed me, maybe it was due to my water sign, Scorpio, trait.

I could smell the steaks Mr. Miller was grilling while I was showering. My stomach began growling. We hadn't had a meal since our peanut butter on rye in the early morning. For dinner Mrs. Miller had also made baked potatoes, tossed salad, and dinner rolls. Paul and I felt like we were in heaven. It was difficult to take my time eating and not chow down everything in minutes. I began to think that if I continued living here I could put on enough weight to play football.

"Tell us about your adventures, Sean, you must have met some interesting people along the way?" asked Mr. Miller.

Most people, especially older adults, thought because of my quiet nature I was a nice young man who was polite, never did anything wrong, and was mature for my age. Some of that may have been true, but there were times where I was out of control or took chances, made uncharacteristic decisions, and did things people never could have imagined.

I had to think carefully about which parts of our trip thus far I should tell the Millers to help both maintain that perception and not make them worried: getting high with Jeff and Julie, no: Mary Ann who wanted to take us back and party all night...no: sleeping on the sides of Interstates, maybe not: the drunk army duo...hmm, no: the VW van criminals...definitely not. The best option, I decided, was to adjust the stories a bit, to tell some fiblets, almost the truth, but a few details missing or changed.

"We've been fortunate enough to have met some good people. A friend of Paul's took us a couple of hours down the road on his way to Yellowstone for the summer. Later we had a tough time getting rides and that's when we changed to taking Interstate 70 instead of I-90 like we originally planned. A young couple took us through some of Ohio, then a woman actually drove us through Indianapolis, a man who worked for the government drove us a long way, from Terre Haute to eastern Kansas City. The next day an off-duty officer only drove us a couple of hours, but had us stop and eat at a great barbecue restaurant in a small town to the west of Kansas City. Let's see... then two Army guys picked us up, and later, another really nice woman drove us from mid-Kansas to Bennett, where you met us. It has worked out reasonably well, I guess."

"Where did you sleep though, motels?" asked Mrs. Miller.

This time Paul answered. "A couple of people let us stay at their place and we camped along the way." Obviously Paul caught my drift of not quite telling the whole truth. "It's been quite an experience, but we still have a long way to go."

"Well, I don't understand it at all," she said. "But I guess that's what some young people do nowadays. It seems risky, that's what I think."

"It's not something I would do if I were a woman, it does seem it would be quite a risk for them, sadly, but Paul and I can physically take care of ourselves," I replied.

Mr. Miller added, "Remember, Jean, when I finished flight school and before leaving for overseas I just had to see you? I hitched rides from the base in Dayton, Ohio to Rochester to spend two days with you. It turned out to be faster than taking a bus and I didn't have the money to pay for a commercial airline seat or train."

She smiled and said, "how could you help yourself, I was quite a catch."

"Yes you were, and still are."

After dinner Paul and I helped clean up the dishes, at least as much as Mrs. Miller would let us. I thought Mrs. Miller seemed to be warming up to us a little bit; maybe the pool filter had cleaned out all of our road filth. I headed to my room early, writing about some of our adventures in my journal before passing out in the ultra-comfortable bed.

A homemade pancake breakfast with real maple syrup gave us a jump start to the morning. I don't know why Mr. Miller didn't weigh fifty pounds more with his wife's fantastic meals, no wonder he swam laps one or more times a day. We dressed for the lower mountain temperatures, me in overalls, flannel shirt and boots, Paul in jeans and his geology club shirt.

Mr. Miller said, "Let's take a drive up through Estes Park to Rocky Mountain National Park. Paul, you might be able to do some rock hunting at different places along the drive. We can also stop at the Ore Cart Rock shop or the Red Rose Rock shop in Estes Park. They carry everything from meteorites, fossils, and jewelry, to agates and geodes. Sean, you should be able to get some great photographs."

"That sounds fantastic, I can't wait to get into the mountains," Paul replied enthusiastically.

The landscape on the drive was exhilarating. In Brockport we had the dirty Barge Canal. We had to drive four hours to get to the Adirondack Mountains, which were beautiful, but just foothills out here. It was nice to sit back and enjoy the scenery without worrying about other passengers or the competency of the driver. Estes Park was only an hour from the Miller's home. We came to a mutual decision to continue into Rocky Mountain National Park via Trail Ridge Road to Grand Lake. The road quickly climbed from over 4,800 feet at Windsor to 7,500 feet at Estes Park. Driving toward Grand Lake we made it to over 12,000 feet. I'd never been in mountains like this before. It was a bit scary for a flatlander like me to see the drop-offs down the mountainsides, but Mr. Miller seemed to have no issues with driving in the altitude. We stopped at several observation pull-offs for photographs and were amazed at seeing Wyoming to the north, the Great Plains to the east, and many high peaks of the Rockies to the south and west. We were being blessed with great, rain-free weather.

Near Milner Pass it was twenty degrees colder than Windsor and much windier. I had to wear my poncho over a corduroy shirt to stay warm whenever we got out of the car to view the sites. We were at the Continental Divide, almost 11,000 feet elevation. During the ride to Grand Lake in the distance we saw elk, deer, and Bighorn sheep. It was an extraordinary experience for Paul and myself. Surprisingly, Mrs. Miller had packed a picnic style lunch, fried chicken, bottles of Coke, potato salad, and homemade brownies, which we all devoured at Point Park in Grand Lake. It didn't seem like this day could get any better. I used up an entire cartridge of film in one day.

Three hours later, reaching Estes Park again, we stopped at two rock shops where Paul purchased several small items, including pieces of banded gold and black gneiss and a green schist. The geology nerd was in heaven.

Reaching the Miller's home late in the day, Mr. Miller changed into his swimsuit to do laps for the second time that day and Paul and I wore our cutoffs again, though this time they were clean. After doing fifty-five push-ups and crunches, which Mr. Miller happily did with us, we joined him in the pool with a Coors beer for each of us that we sipped in-between laps. Well, Mr. Miller and Paul sipped between laps, I was comfortable floating on my back in the pool and staying within arm's length of my Coors. Mrs. Miller seemed happier, more relaxed around us now, and made a dinner of roast beef, mashed potatoes, green beans, and fresh baked rolls, a true home-style, comfort food meal, while we swam. Considering how thin she was, my guess was she swam quite a bit, but was too modest to do so while a couple of nineteen year old young men were around.

"Since you're leaving tomorrow, we can drive up to Casper, Wyoming, give you a bit of a head start toward Yellowstone, will that help?" asked Mr. Miller, adding with a smile, "Unless you want to stay in Windsor, I can help you get a job at the plant."

I knew Mr. Miller well enough that the offer was only partly made in jest and that he had probably talked with my Dad about it beforehand. Dad seemed pissed off already that I took off for this hitchhiking trip instead of taking a summer job at Kodak in Rochester. If Dad really had his way I'd be at Camp Lejeune partaking in Marine Corps boot camp. What did it matter to him, though, I paid for my own tuition and books; no money was coming out of his pocket for my college expenses.

"I appreciate it, Mr. Miller," I answered, while grabbing another dinner roll. "Maybe in the future I could come back and work here, this is a beautiful area of the country, I can see why you two moved to Windsor. I'm kind of amazed my father didn't take a job here."

"What about you, Paul, any interest in moving here now?"

"There's some interest, such fantastic geological history, it's wonderful out here," he said. "But I want to complete my last two years at Brockport, play football in the fall and get my bachelor's degree in geology. Maybe after graduating I'll come out to this area again."

A lazy night after the travels of the day was most welcome by me. After writing in my journal I conked out early and slept for over eight hours without waking once, which was extremely unusual. Another round of sit-ups and push-ups by Paul, Mr. Miller, and me was followed by a stomach filling breakfast. Mr. and Mrs. Miller shared cooking duties of eggs, toast, bacon, and home fries. After that feast we got in the Bonneville and headed to Casper, Wyoming, about three hours away. Mrs. Miller gave each of us a lunch bag with a ham and cheese sandwich, an apple, and two homemade chocolate chip cookies. Both Millers seemed really hesitant about leaving us on the side of the road near the Interstate 25 on-ramp, and truthfully, I was going to miss their hospitality and the comfort of the great meals, indoor pool, and a clean bed. From all the great food it felt like I had put on five pounds in less than three days.

I began thinking working in Windsor may not be a bad idea. Hell, I was still confused about what to major in at Brockport, maybe earning money at Kodak out here and exploring the mountains would be a good change in my life.

"It was nice staying at the Millers, Sean, but sometimes it seemed more like being with our parents. Wouldn't it have been nice to hit a bar or something one of the nights?"

"I guess, yeah, but I didn't mind the food, pool, or seeing Rocky Mountain National Park. It was nice to get a bit of a break from sleeping on the side of the road."

"Yeah, okay, sure, I guess so, whatever, let's get going and see if we can get another ride."

It was Friday, July 2, around noon. The day was sunny, already seventy degrees, I was dressed in my now clean cutoff shorts, socks, hiking boots, my green SUNY Brockport Earth Science t-shirt, and my Rochester Red Wing baseball hat. Paul had a similar outfit, except for a Brockport football jersey he had cut the sleeves off of and no hat. He always thought his thick, golden blonde hair would attract women and help us get a ride. Who was I to argue? There was something to be said about looking like a younger version of Robert Redford.

Wild Bill Cody

People in the middle of Wyoming didn't seem friendly to hitchhikers waiting at their on-ramp for a ride. Maybe because it was a holiday weekend, families were going to see loved ones or get to a vacation spot, whatever, they sure didn't want to pick up two guys from the roadside. Where were the Millers? Let me go back to the pool and home cooked meals. I'll apply for a job at Kodak right now. I don't care, I'll drive a forklift, be a security guard; it wouldn't matter. I could be hiking every weekend. This was not much fun. Paul and I ate the lunches Mrs. Miller had packed to help pass time, except I had to take the cheese off my sandwich. Yuck. I continued reading *On the Road*. Finally, four hours after being left by the Millers, a 1974 dark blue Ford Granada pulled over.

The middle-aged, balding male driver, he looked a bit like William Conrad from the television show *Cannon*, leaned over to the window and said, "Where are you two heading?"

"Yellowstone National Park, we have a friend who is starting a full-time job there training to be a park ranger, we want to visit, maybe do some camping and hiking on our own too," said Paul.

"I can get you to Cody; you'll have to find another ride after that."

"That's fine with us," I replied.

The man got out and opened the trunk for our packs. I recognized the scent of English Leather on him. He was wearing dress pants, a button down long sleeve shirt and penny loafers. He had a couple of suitcases and two small boxes in the trunk, but still room for our packs. I took the shotgun seat and Paul sat in the back. Paul had checked his map and realized it was about three and a half hours to Cody, putting us in the town around eight p.m.

"I'm Dale, Dale Barlow, what are your names?" he asked as we began to merge onto Interstate 25.

It was interesting that Paul and I were so honest it never crossed our minds to lie to people about our names. We put our trust in people and assumed they would trust us, except the VW bus criminals, they were a different story and worthy of suspicion.

77

"I'm Sean, in the back is Paul," I replied. "He's a football playing geology major and I'm an English major, I think, that could change. Are you a doctor?"

"What did you say that for?" demanded Mr. Barlow, his face turning to a scowl.

"I'm sorry, I saw your hospital papers on the seat between us, medical equipment and catalogs and such and assumed you were a doctor."

"There are a lot of jobs in the medical field besides being a doctor," he replied, still a bit of anger evident in his voice.

"I didn't mean anything by it, I was being curious, that's all. One of the best things about hitchhiking is finding out about all the types of jobs available from the people who pick us up."

"I'm a salesman; I contact doctors and administrators in hospitals and at their offices, trying to sell them medical equipment." He was beginning to calm down a bit.

"That seems interesting," said Paul, rescuing me from an awkward conversation. "One thing we've learned on our travels from New York is the different types of careers people have," reinforcing what I had said. It's been educational for us, to say the least. I still have two years left before graduating and Sean, probably three, but we never know about him, dropping in and out of college on a whim, it seems."

"Hey, I'm doing okay now. I just completed a full year of classes."

"It's progress, a small step in the right direction," Paul said sarcastically.

Mr. Barlow seemed to grow a bit friendlier as the ride continued. We stopped for gas at the Union 76 station in Thermopolis, a truly weird sounding town, not knowing we were passing up an opportunity to spend the night and enjoy hot springs, petroglyphs, and dinosaur fossils. Paul and I took turns going into the station for some snacks, since the food Mrs. Miller had packed was long gone. Mr. Barlow seemed trustworthy, but leaving our only belongings with a complete stranger didn't seem like a great idea. It was always difficult to fully trust people we had just met, especially after our VW van experience. I bought a twelve ounce can of Coke, a box of mini-doughnuts, a package of Lance peanut butter crackers, and, for a new supply of gorp; a small bag of pretzels, dried fruit, a jar of peanuts, and a big bag of M&M's. Paul surprised me, buying two Hostess snowball snacks, a lemonade, and the biggest chocolate chip raisin filled cookie I had ever seen. It definitely wasn't his typical health food meal.

It was a partly cloudy night, the moon and stars struggling to break through when we finally drove into Cody. We passed by several Mom and Pop type small motels. The large chain motels must not have thought Cody was worthy of their business, despite Yellowstone being an hour away.

Mr. Barlow said, "I'm dropping you two off outside of town, then coming back to find a room. I don't need to take the chance of you knowing where I am, never can be too trusting. I do thank you for the company on the trip from Casper though; it made the hours go by a bit quicker."

"We understand, Mr. Barlow, that makes sense, and we appreciate the ride, thanks," said Paul.

I got out of the Granada and took the packs from the trunk. Paul and I watched Mr. Barlow do a U-turn and head back to town. Why we didn't ask to be dropped off at one of the small motels was a mystery to me. I guess without even talking to each other we knew we were too cheap to spend twenty dollars, or whatever, on a room. It was easy to second guess decisions made on our trip, but there wasn't always time or opportunities to consider all of the alternatives thoroughly. It was 8:30 p.m. and we began looking for a dry, soft spot in the dirt and weeds to lie down on away from people in cars or trucks being able to see us as they drove on Route 14. I also wasn't thrilled about seeing any gopher holes, or worse, elk, grizzlies, moose or wolves that might get curious about what we were doing out there.

Paul teasingly said, "Remember Sean, rattlers like warm bodies, you might want to make sure they don't join you in the sleeping bag." Sometimes he really annoyed me, but my fear of snakes drove me to zip my bag so tight an ant couldn't get inside. Paul shook his head and laughed, "It's like seventy-five degrees still; you're going to sweat to death."

"Better than a snake bite! You want to suck the venom out of me?" I was laying on my back, my head resting on Atlas, and thinking about our travels thus far while staring at the stars and moon between the clouds floating by, when sleep overcame me.

***

Fear, doubt, invading

Wind bends doesn't break willow

Faith in survival

I was six years old the first time I remember going out to explore the country. The line of tall poplar trees gently swaying in the summer breeze seemed far away from our house on Westwood Drive, an adventurous trek that James, my nine year old brother and I, felt sure we could handle. Mom didn't seem quite as confident but agreed to let us go. The poplars must have been at least two miles from our house, past some farm fields and smaller growth of trees. Mom came out of the house with two Hostess cupcakes, four homemade chocolate chip cookies, my Bullwinkle thermos and James's Jetsons thermos both filled with ice cold cherry Kool-Aid and placed them in a knapsack James carried. She waved goodbye and probably secretly thought we would turn around soon, but didn't discourage us from the trip.

It was a hot, cloudless, humid, sticky August day, typical of Brockport in the summer. James and I began our trek easily enough through the suburban neighborhood backyards until finally reaching the first field. Mom was already out of sight. Sweat soon began to work its way through our shirts and shorts. Brambles stuck to our socks and Keds sneakers. We climbed over small fallen trees, through uncut knee high grass and cornfields with stalks leering over our heads. The poplar trees never seemed to get any closer.

James had never ending patience, for me, the weather, bugs, and other people. It was a quality that made me get frustrated even faster since I had no patience at all and couldn't understand why he wasn't the same.

The bugs began a relentless attack on our necks, faces, arms, and ears, especially mine. I seemed to attract the beasts like no other person in existence. Wasps and yellow jackets, which I was allergic to, were particularly attracted to me. It was a merciless assault under which we had little defense. I began slapping at them, my arms twirling in circles like an out of control airplane propeller.

"Would you stop that?" James said. "It won't help."

"The bugs are driving me crazy, why aren't they biting you too?" I yelled, and began running through the cornfield to find refuge.

James caught up with me as we came to a small clearing and a stone fence that was perfect to climb on and sit for a while. A gentle breeze came up and helped keep the bugs at bay. We sat in silence for several minutes, looking ahead to the poplar trees and behind to the safety of our house. We agreed to turn around and head back home after first having some Kool-Aid and a cupcake. I had been defeated by the distance, bugs, and heat. James was defeated by my complaints and together we began the long trudge back.

Mom was in the backyard "working", no doubt really watching to see where we would end up or get lost and have to be rescued. She pulled out an old blanket from the house and placed it under our giant willow tree. James and I finished our cookies and ate peanut butter and strawberry jelly sandwiches in silence. The journey may not have been a complete success, but it gave me a taste of leaving the nest. We moved from that house a year later, never having another opportunity to travel to the poplars or embrace the safety of the willow tree again.

***

I woke with a start, looking around through the night and quickly realizing I must have gone off on one of my weird dreams again. At times my dreams seemed so intense, so real, it took a minute to come back to reality. The nightmares I had every other week or so would wake me when I began screaming from being trapped in some room or maze, in the midst of dying, or escaping from some evil force. Paul was snoring a few feet away from me, a gentle breeze was blowing the tall grass keeping bugs at bay. It didn't appear any animals had caught our scent and were going to try and eat us anytime soon. I checked my wrist watch, it was only four in the morning, a few white puffy clouds were now floating in the sky, no traffic sounds could be heard on the highway, and I quickly fell back asleep.

In the morning we shook out our stiffness from sleeping on the ground by doing sixty push-ups, but skipped the sit-ups to avoid making more of a mess of our clothes. I changed into my Poe t-shirt with the flannel shirt over it and overalls to fight off the morning chill. For breakfast we shared the Hostess mini-donuts I had bought at the Union 76 station, packed our gear, with me carefully looking for snakes in my sleeping bag, walked the hundred yards to the roadway, climbed over the guardrail, and hoped for the best. There were lots of rock outcroppings nearby, which led Paul to grab his rock pick and explore, leaving me to place our "WEST" sign propped against Atlas and hold my thumb out. Would drivers think it was just me hitchhiking? Who knew, but it did seem Paul could have waited for a better time to hunt rocks. Of course ten minutes later he came back with a smile plastered across his face holding an agate and a piece of granite, which he placed in his pack.

A ride into Yellowstone wasn't coming quickly. Dozens of cars passed by, but no one would stop for us. I had the awesome idea to hold my yellow poncho as Paul held up a large stone, hoping someone might get our sense of humor. It was another hour before a red 1973 Datsun station wagon stopped. An elderly man, he must have been at least sixty-five, wearing a white button down sweater and blue jeans, got out of the passenger seat and a gray haired woman who seemed the same age came over to us from the driver's seat, wearing hiking boots, jeans, a flowery blouse and lightweight tan jacket zipped halfway up.

Yellowstone at Last

"We stopped because Carol liked the clue to where you are heading, very cute holding the rock and yellow poncho," said the bald, bespectacled, old man who was holding a small black dog in his arms. "Where in the park do you want to get to today?"

"We're going to meet a friend who's working at Mammoth Hot Springs training to be a park ranger. He graduated from college in late May, in Upstate New York," said Paul.

"Today is your lucky day; we have a cabin reserved up there. It's going to take about four hours to drive there if we don't stop to see any attractions along the way, but we really would like to see Old Faithful, so the trip may take longer. Of course you don't have to ride with us the entire way if you're in a hurry. Where are you staying?"

"With luck we can stay in the worker's dorm, but if not we have a tent and will go to the campground," replied Paul. "And we'd love to see Old Faithful, when you're hitchhiking you can't be in a hurry since we're always relying on other people."

"We have a lot of luggage and supplies in the car, as you can see, not to mention Darwin, our little beagle, so you're going to have to keep your packs with you and squeeze into the backseat," said the man. "By the way, my name is Jim, we are Jim and Carol Jefferson, and you two are called?"

"Oh, sorry, I'm Paul Davis, he's Sean Matheson. We're college students from Brockport, New York, near Rochester."

"Home of Kodak, we know where Rochester is," said Jim.

"Well, nice to meet you, buckle up and let's get going," said Carol. "I'm anxious to see the park." From the rear view mirror a scented pine tree hung down. A small bag was between Paul and me on the floor for garbage. Darwin sat up front on Jim's lap.

"What are your college majors?" asked Jim.

"I'm trying to combine earth science with English," I answered. "Maybe I'll be able to get a job in technical writing or magazine articles on science, I'm really not sure."

"I'm a geology major," Paul said. "Probably headed for a job in the oil or gas industry."

"So you both must have done well with science classes in high school?"

"I aced mine," said Paul.

"I actually struggled a bit, especially with biology, but for some reason still found them fascinating," I said.

"Oh, I see. Well Carol and I recently retired from teaching. I was a high school biology teacher and Carol was a fifth grade teacher, usually, though she had to switch grades a few times during her thirty-five year career."

"Biology, hmm, I could have used you for that class," I said. "I was flunking for two quarters before putting in a little more effort and staying after school every day to catch up on all the labs I had, umm, neglected to complete. My parents made it clear if I was going to play sports again that year then I had to pass biology. My teacher was really mean to me for weeks until I stayed after school and began doing some work, and then he relaxed his grip a bit."

"Sounds like he cared a lot about your success and others if he always stayed after school hours. He wasn't required to do that, you know. Maybe he knew he had to push you, that you had it in yourself to succeed if you just put some effort into it. Plus, look at you now, majoring in science, maybe you owe him a big thanks."

"That could be true, I think he would be surprised I've made it this far in the sciences, but he sure was nasty to me for a long time, always calling on me to answer questions in class when he knew I wouldn't know the answer. It was embarrassing, I would begin to sweat just walking into his classroom and when he did ask me a question I'd squirm in my seat and my face would turn red. It wasn't fun and made me hate going to biology class."

"Where did you teach at, what city or town?" asked Paul, trying to change the subject a little.

"Oh, we're from Pennsylvania, Scranton to be exact; a few hours from Rochester. We've been retired for three years and take a different road trip each summer. This time, obviously, is Yellowstone, and in a week or so we'll head up to Glacier National Park before weaving our way back home."

Carol continued driving on Route 14-16-20, which was a bit confusing since it seemed to be the same road, just the numbers changed. Jim occasionally checked his Rand-McNally road map, but there wasn't really any reason to since this was the main road to Yellowstone from Cody. From signs on the highway it was better known as The Buffalo Bill Scenic Byway through Buffalo Bill State Park, then went through the East Entrance of Yellowstone, about fifty miles from Cody. It wasn't a fast trip, which I was okay with, such beautiful, mountainous surroundings with lush forests, part of the Shoshone National Forest area, passing white pine and spruce trees. We continued around Yellowstone Lake to Route 20, with a short stop at the West Thumb geyser basin, before going onto Route 191, also called Grand Loop road, and finally to Old Faithful. The size of Yellowstone Park amazed me and we were only seeing a tiny piece of it from the roadway and scenic pull-offs.

Carol parked the Datsun as close to the visitor center as she could. All four of us, with Jim still carrying Darwin, headed to the closest viewing area to the geyser we could get to through the crowds of people. I still had twelve photos left on my third role of film and strapped the camera around my neck, anxiously waiting for the geyser to erupt. When it finally did less than an hour later, it was mesmerizing. Seeing the geyser in photographs or on television was one thing, in person it was taking it to an entirely different level. I managed to snap four photographs, including one with Paul standing facing me and Old Faithful erupting behind him. Carol and Jim had Paul take their photograph using a Nikon Nikomat SLR camera, a bit higher quality than my Kodak Instamatic. Before getting back in the Datsun I ate my Lance peanut butter crackers and gorp while Paul polished off his Hostess Snowballs. I was beginning to think peanut butter ran through my veins.

It was now around three p.m. and we had fifty miles to drive before reaching Mammoth Hot Springs, maybe an hour; if there weren't any unexpected stops for wildlife, mountains, or geysers. I wasn't necessarily in a rush to see Richard Randall and his Land Cruiser again, but having a place to stay and a person who was knowledgeable about the area as we explored Mammoth for a few nights was something to look forward to.

Jim took over the driving so Carol could sightsee a bit more without driving us off the highway looking for buffalo, elk, birds, or geysers. We arrived in Mammoth Hot Springs around five p.m., gave our thanks to the Jeffersons and wished them well on the rest of their trip. Paul had Richard's dorm address so we picked up our packs and headed toward the building.

Mammoth Hot Springs

We walked over to the Spruce Dorm, entered through the main door, and, knowing Richard lived on the second floor, headed there. No one bothered us or seemed to care that we were wandering around the dorm. We looked in the rooms that had open doors as we searched for Richard, calling his name several times. The rooms were large, but sparsely furnished, similar to a college dorm. There were two bunks in each room with a small dresser for each person. A community bathroom was centrally located on each of the two floors. This was one of many housing units for summer employees at Yellowstone. Richard was in Room 214, the only person currently living in that room.

"Hey, you guys made it," he said enthusiastically, jumping up from his bed. "Welcome to Mammoth," and he shook our hands.

"Thanks, glad to be here," said Paul.

"Put your packs in my room, you can each have a bunk, okay?"

"Sounds great," I said, and placed Atlas on a bottom bunk. "Hey, I'm going to check out the bathroom, I'll be right back."

When I returned Paul and Richard were talking about each other's adventures getting to Yellowstone. Richard had only arrived on Thursday since he spent two nights with relatives near Chicago and with twenty hours to drive after that, spent a night in Mitchell, South Dakota, renowned home of the Corn Palace. From everything I had read it was a tourist trap. Every year the locals stuck corn cobs in different designs on a wooden structure and invited the public inside to learn everything there was to know about corn. It wasn't a place I ever felt the need to visit, but out in the middle of nowhere, it was a last chance for gas or a Big Mac for miles and miles.

"Guess, what?" Richard said. "Remember how I dropped you off in Fredonia because of the noise in my Toyota? It turns out it wasn't from you guys after all. I kept hearing it to the Pennsylvania border and stopped at the first rest area. The noise was driving me crazy. My own backpack and a suitcase were rubbing against each other. Stupid, right? But I knew you two could handle the hitchhiking, that's really what you started the trip for anyhow, right?"

All I could think was, you fucking idiot, we could have had a ride all the way to Chicago, been there Sunday night instead of weaving our way to a different Interstate, sleeping in the grass off of a couple of highways, riding with church robbers, but noooo, you kicked us out for nothing.

Fortunately Paul answered, "No problem, as I was telling you we met quite a few interesting people, it all worked out pretty well."

"Good. Let's go over to the dining hall, I'm hungry and betting you guys are too. I get a discounted rate as an employee, you two will have to pay full retail price. Sorry about that."

"Sounds like a great idea, I'm starving, and we're good with paying the regular price," I said.

When dinner was finished Richard took us on a tour of some of the Mammoth sites, including walking on the boardwalk near the hydrothermal features. The two geologist majors were in their glory discussing the limestone, travertine, and geothermal formations; it was like being back in a geology class. I was disgusted by the rotten egg smell coming from the thermal features, but was still able to enjoy the uniqueness of the area; the limestone and travertine terraces, including Minerva Terrace. I used up a roll of film during the walk listening to the information these two rock nerds were sharing.

Afterward, since it was Saturday night and many of the summer workers had the night off, Richard told us we'd be going to the Iron Horse Saloon in nearby Gardiner, Montana for drinking and dancing. He promised many of the female workers, who lived in the nearby Juniper Hall dorm, would be going there to party. Paul and I changed from our grubby hitchhiking clothes, and, thanks to Mrs. Miller, had clean, decent stuff to wear. I put on overalls with my Edgar Allen Poe t-shirt, clean socks, sneakers, and my Rochester Red Wing hat, with my thick, curly brown hair sticking out. Paul wore his Levi's, sneakers, and a Brockport State t-shirt. Gardiner was a short five mile drive from Mammoth via the North Entrance Road, past the Boiling River hot springs, with a view of the Gallatin Range and paralleling the Gardiner River.

The Iron Horse was hopping when we walked through the door. Girls and guys were scattered throughout the bar. The air was thick from cigarette smoke and hamburger grease, the floor covered in peanut shells. The brown paneled walls were decorated with Hamm's, Pabst, Coors, and Schaefer neon beer signs, elk and deer antlers, a couple of moose heads, and a bearskin hung from the rafters. The bar top was so long at least thirty people were sitting at it, booths and tables were spread throughout the space, all filled with an eclectic mix of townies, cowboy wannabes, tourists, and Yellowstone employees. There were two United Ball Bowler machines, four pinball machines, a pool table, and a dance floor at the far end. They had everything here and I felt at home. The jukebox was playing "You're No Good," by Linda Ronstadt as we walked up to the bar to order drinks. Richard was nice enough to buy our first round, which for me was a double shot rum and Coke. I needed to up my courage quotient quickly if I was going to make conversation with one of the girls in the bar and eventually ask one to dance with me.

The first drink went down quickly, and with my second I began to relax and wandered over to the pool table where a couple of guys were dressed like cowboys. One was wearing a red plaid corduroy shirt with a pack of Tareyton cigarettes in his pocket. His black cowboy hat was pushed back slightly on his head, which helped accentuate his ungodly thick, black eyebrows. The other guy was in a blue denim work shirt and had the biggest belt buckle I had ever seen, which included a bucking bronco emblazoned design. Both were wearing Lee jeans that were so tight I couldn't imagine how they had pulled them on, all that was missing from these two were spurs on their boots. They were playing a game of eight ball, which judging by the balls being sunk, Big Buckle was clearly better at. I could always use extra drinking money, so I thought hustling the locals would be a good way of earning a few bucks.

"Mind if I play the winner?" I asked. They looked me up and down and snickered seeing me with my thick, shoulder length brown hair sticking out of my baseball cap and wearing a Poe shirt. I'm pretty sure they had no idea who Edgar Allen Poe was.
"Why should we let you play?" replied Big Buckle cowboy, taking a puff from his Lucky Strike cigarette.

"It could be a good way for you to earn a few bucks, or me, if I'm lucky."

"You some kind of hustler?"

"Nah, not me, but I am willing to take my chances at beating you. How about the best two out of three games of eight ball, ten dollars to the winner? Look, I'm already working on my fourth shot of rum, my hands aren't that steady anymore." I stuck my hand out and let my fingers shake a bit knowing that my second double shot of rum and Coke barely had an effect. I had built up quite a tolerance for alcohol over the past eighteen months.

"Sure, put your ten spot on the table, I'll do the same, and let's play, but I'm breaking first," said Mr. Big Buckle.

"Here you go, fine by me, go ahead and break, but I get to break for the second game."

Mr. Big Buckle had a nice break and got a ball in the pocket. He put in two more before missing. Maybe he did know how to play, but that would make victory even sweeter. I sunk four in a row before missing a tough bank shot. We traded shots before Mr. Big Buckle won the game.

"Nice game, guess I have to beat you in the next two," I said. "Want to put an extra ten on the outcome?"

"Twenty to the winner? Why not? Easy money."

Mr. Big Buckle pulled out his wallet and laid down another ten and I did the same, placing our money under my rum and Coke glass after taking a nice long drink. This game began a little differently as I broke and put in four straight balls. Big Buckle sank only one before missing. I ran the table and won easily. The two cowboys looked at each other nervously and stopped making jokes about my overalls and Poe shirt, or maybe it had to do with Richard and Paul coming over to have a look at the proceedings, bringing me a third drink for good luck. The deciding game had Mr. Big Buckle break but no balls went in. Bad luck on his part. I calmly walked around the table making shot after shot, there must have been something special in the rum at the Iron Horse Saloon or maybe I was feeling extra sharp that night. After winning I took the money, finished my drink, and tried to shake their hands, but the cowboys wanted nothing more to do with me.

"Thanks for the game, guys, enjoy the rest of your night!"

This time it was my turn to buy the round of drinks and I walked up to the bar feeling full of myself, enough so that I squeezed in between two ladies to order. When the bartender came over I looked at the brunette on my right and the other one on my left and asked, "Can I buy you two ladies a drink?"

"Why not," said the one on my right. "I'll have a Margarita, what do you want Donna?"

"Oh, how about another Tequila Sunrise," she stated.

"No problem," I said, and gave the bartender the five drink order. When he brought them over I handed the Margarita to the brunette on my right and asked for her name. "Marcia" was the one word answer. I wasn't getting a warm friendly feeling but the rum was working its magic on me as the jukebox blasted out a Billy Preston song, "Nothing from Nothing."

"What jobs do you two have at Mammoth?" I asked.

"We both work in guest services at the hotel," said Donna. "What do you do?"

For a moment I thought about lying, there were so many college students working at Yellowstone, they wouldn't have known the difference; maybe I would get lucky with one of them if they thought I was going to be around all summer. Unfortunately my morals took over, even on my fifth drink, through my blurry eyes, and I told the truth about being from New York and that I would only be staying in the area for a few days. Donna looked disappointed. I was only saved by the Beatles "Twist and Shout" coming over the speakers and asked Marcia if she wanted to dance, took her hand, and headed to the dance floor.

While I did my best twisting Marcia looked a bit annoyed and as we walked back to the bar said, "I'm not into the facial expressions while dancing."

Until then I really didn't think about what my face looked like when dancing. I was always more concerned about tripping over my feet, stepping on my partner's toes, or lack of rhythm. A former girlfriend had told me every movement had meaning, but didn't mention my face had issues. Now I had one more thing to worry

91

about. My dancing was done for the night. I sat down next to Donna as Marcia went off to dance with Mr. Big Buckle.

"I'm sorry about her," said Donna. "She can be a little insensitive."

"Whatever, I should have asked you to dance, that was a mistake, I'm sorry," and with that I downed my drink and ordered another round. "Would you dance with me if a song comes on I might be able to move my feet without tripping you? I'll try not to make weird faces."

"Hah, I'm not much of a dancer either," Donna said. "But I'd love to." A couple of songs later Ray Charles' "I Got a Woman" song came on and we got up and fumbled our way through it together. We stayed on the dance floor for a slow song, "You are so Beautiful" by Joe Cocker. When I got closer to Donna there was a sweet, delicate smell of honey. I placed my arms around her, which helped as much with my balance as feeling good about touching a woman for the first time in months. When the song ended we went back to the bar for glasses of water and a bowl of beer nuts, opting to play a few games of bowling instead of having any more alcohol.

The night ended peacefully with Richard taking myself, Paul, Donna, and Marcia back to Mammoth. I made faces at Marcia's back as she walked toward the dorm, but was still too buzzed to think about getting Donna's full name or home address so I might be able to contact her sometime in the future. At the Spruce Dorm I collapsed on my bunk, still wearing the same clothes until five a.m., when I managed to stumble to the bathroom and back to bed, stripping down to my underwear before falling asleep again.

Sunday, July 4, I woke up around nine a.m. with my head pounding. My mouth tasted like rum, my clothes and hair smelled like cigarette smoke, I had five dollars in my pants pocket left from the pool winnings, and was so hungry my stomach felt like it was eating its cell walls. I balanced myself against the shower stall as I washed the filth and cigarette smoke off, put on my cutoffs, clean socks, boots, 'keep on truckin' shirt, and Red Wing hat. I was hoping some food would help with the intense headache caused by my hangover, the four aspirin I swallowed didn't seem to be having an effect. Finally, after waiting for them until ten a.m., Paul, Richard, and I headed over to the dining hall for the morning breakfast buffet.

I couldn't seem to get enough of the thick buttermilk pancakes and sausage patties, drowning all of them in maple syrup, each bite soaking up a bit more of the rum from the night before. I secretly hoped to see Donna again, but she was nowhere in sight. I had definitely learned in the past couple of years that there were often missed opportunities in life to make a lasting connection with someone, last night was no exception.

After breakfast Richard was kind enough on his day off to take us on a tour of old Fort Yellowstone at Mammoth Hot Springs and help plan a hiking trip Paul and I would be taking on Monday. We stopped at the general store to stock up on food for our trek: four cans of tuna, a loaf of Wonder white bread, a box of Ritz crackers, jar of peanut butter, a box of Carnation breakfast bars, two apples, and a dozen oatmeal cookies.

The next morning we bought breakfast sandwiches from the dining hall to eat on our way to the trail head. Richard had agreed to drop Paul and me off at the Specimen Ridge Trail before he began work. It was a warm morning with a brilliant sun lighting our way. I wore my gym shorts, hiking boots, Red Wing hat, and earth science club shirt. My camera was draped around my neck in case there was some spectacular scenery or wild animal I wanted to photograph quickly. Paul wore his geology hiking shorts, short sleeve hiking shirt, and boots. The plan was to hike from the trail head, about 2.3 miles, and connect to the Agate Creek Trail, which would take us to the bottom of the Grand Canyon of the Yellowstone, 4.3 miles later, and spend the night in my two man tent. Hiking up and down trails in the wilderness wasn't close to walking through a village, on a track, or along sidewalks. It could easily take an hour to go a mile in the mountains. Paul and I also were warned to keep talking while walking so that any bears might be warned of our presence and not attack us. More than anything else that was what I was worried about, so I kept scanning the tall weeds, wildflowers, and tree line for bears. I had to keep telling Paul to yell or talk, but for someone who usually had no problem with that he seemed reluctant to ruin the wilds of Yellowstone with his voice, and mine he found annoying.

"Yeah Sean, I know you're scared of bears, elk, birds, snakes, and most anything that moves. I don't have to constantly hear about making noise out here, do I? Can't we just enjoy the quiet of this wondrous area, for God's sake?" Paul turned back and yelled at me.

At least he was talking out loud, even if it was in anger. I couldn't sing worth shit, so every few minutes I would randomly yell stupid things. I stopped often for photo opportunities, knowing, even at nineteen, that I would never be here again. The beauty and immensity of Yellowstone was captivating. I couldn't imagine being a frontiersman or soldier in the nineteenth century and one of the first white persons to come across this area, making your own trails, or if lucky, following a Native American path. In mid-afternoon, after seeing only one other person far downstream who was fishing, we found a decent flat area to pitch the tent. For lunch we didn't feel like starting a fire to cook anything; instead I ate crackers dipped in peanut butter and Paul had gorp and an apple. It was too bad neither of us was a fisherman and could try to catch a trout or two, but then we would have needed a fire and probably would have had the fish stolen by a bear.

Nearby was a ravine that Paul thought we should explore; hoping to find some rock or mineral specimens we could take back to New York. We took off climbing up, up, up, scrambling boulders on all fours, balancing on rocks to cross back and forth across the small stream that during spring thaws would have been a raging river. Paul used his pick to get samples of travertine and quartz. After a couple of hours of hiking Paul stumbled onto horns from a bighorn sheep that had been separated from the skull. We weren't sure about the legality of removing the horns from the park, but Paul did carry them back down the ravine and hid them among some boulders near our campsite.

I was a bit nervous sleeping in such a remote area. We had no defense against wild animals except jackknifes, not much of a deterrent for the fox, bear, elk, moose, or mountain lions that might come to the river for water or food. For dinner we ate canned tuna on white bread followed by three cookies apiece. After hiking all day the food wasn't exactly delicious but at least it was filling and semi-nutritious.

"Remember, Paul, we have to put all of our food and waste in the plastic bag and hang it from a tree," I said.

"Yeah, I know, that's three times in the last hour you've said the same thing, you don't have to keep saying it!" Paul yelled.

"Well, I don't feel like having bears, wolves, coyotes or any other animals visiting us during the night. Dark comes early out here in the middle of nowhere and we need to be ready."

"Yeah, yeah, yeah, mister afraid of snakes or almost any other animal. I've seen you duck from birds flying overhead, you'd probably run from a fish if you saw one while wading in the river."

"Depends how big the fish was. If I'm going to die I don't want it to be from being mauled to death by some animal. So let's get the bag tied up and ready for bed."

We were tired from hiking and soon after dark went into the tent, neither of us having trouble falling asleep. I woke up several times during the night, sure that I heard animals outside our tent but too scared to confront them. One bear paw across the tent would have destroyed it, then what? Run to the river? Climb a tree? Play dead? I was faster than Paul in distances longer than a quarter mile, but in sprints he'd win and the bear would maul me for a late night snack. One or both of us would be in pieces, probably dead. Fortunately I didn't have to go out for my usual middle of the night pee; sometimes being dehydrated was a good thing.

Paul and I woke at sunrise Tuesday morning. I was running short on clean clothes so I only changed my underwear and socks before putting my earth science shirt and gym shorts back on from the day before. A little extra deodorant helped hide the shirt stench. We ate two Carnation bars apiece and finished off the cookies while hiking out of the river area. Paul carried the horns up the Agate Creek Trail before hiding them behind some boulders in the tall grass. It was mostly uphill; but since we knew the way now it went fairly quickly. Paul still wouldn't talk much on the trail, so I took to singing in my off-key voice every Beatles tune I knew. One was "Blackbird Singing in the Dead of Night", which I kept repeating over and over again.

"Jesus Sean, would you please sing something else? I'm going to fetch a bear myself just so it shuts you up!"

We had to hitchhike from the trail head back to Richard's dorm. When we arrived there he informed us his supervisor said we could no longer stay in the dorm as it was reserved for employees only. Of course I wasn't totally surprised by the decision by Richard's boss, that's the kind of thing bosses have to do, but it was still disappointing. Paul and I moved down to the Mammoth campground, pitching the tent in a nice flat area not far from the bathrooms. Paul mentioned to Richard about the sheep horns he had found.

"Those can be valuable, you should have carried them out to the road and back here."

"How could I, when I didn't know who would give us a ride back to Mammoth?" asked Paul.

"Well, let's go back now, you can hike back quickly and bring them out."

"Yeah, I guess, but we have to leave immediately," said Paul. "I don't want to be out there alone in the dark trying to stay on the trail."

Richard drove us back to the trail head. Paul took off, not carrying his backpack, only taking a canteen of water, the remaining two Carnation bars, and a bag of gorp. He began by jogging down the path. At least this time he knew where he was going. Richard and I sat in the Toyota to wait. Three hours later Richard said, "If I thought it would take this long I would have gone back to the dorm and come out later."

"It's a pretty good hike," I said. "It's not like he put them really close to the road."

It was dusk when Paul finally appeared from the wilderness with the horns intact. He slowly climbed, obviously exhausted, into the back seat of the Cruiser and Richard drove to the dorm. He hid the horns in his room and Paul and I stopped at the general store for a six-pack of cold Schmidt's Tiger Ale, two Hostess fruit pies, and two souvenir Yellowstone National Park shirts before continuing to the campground, polishing off a can apiece while walking there. The cold Schmidt's tasted so freaking good after a couple of long days on the trails. For dinner we ate tuna on white bread sandwiches again, with cookies and fruit pies as side dishes while finishing our six-pack.

Wednesday morning Paul and I were able to sneak back into the dorm and toss our well-worn clothes into two washers. I had to go commando and put on my new Yellowstone shirt and sneakers without socks as we took another walk around historic Fort Yellowstone while our clothes were in the dryer. Once again I wished that I had made the choice to work at one of the national parks like Yellowstone. It seemed like the natural choice of a career for me instead of ending up sitting in an office at some factory. Why couldn't I ever make up my freaking mind and stay focused on one goal for more than a few months? It was wonderful being in Wyoming, so different from Western New York. Quiet, peaceful, insanely tall mountain peaks, trails, fresh air, so much to see, it would take weeks, months, to absorb it all. I was jealous of the experience these college students were having, what a life changing event for them.

After packing away our clean clothes, we went to the dining hall for a quick burger, Coke, and fries before hiking the Bunsen Peak Trail for views of Swan Lake Flats, the Gallatin Mountain Range, and the Mammoth Hot Springs area. The three hour hike was a great way to spend our last day at Yellowstone. When he finished work Richard drove us back to the Iron Horse Saloon for a couple of beers and dinner of fried chicken, greasy fries and sourdough rolls. The three of us mutually agreed to leave early, before the alcohol took over our brains again and knowing we had to get up early Thursday to head back out on the road.

At sunrise I dressed in nice smelling clean underwear, cutoff shorts, socks, a white t-shirt, and because it was still a bit cool still, a flannel shirt. My boots were tied to Atlas and canteens filled with fresh mountain water. Paul and I packed up the tent and met Richard at the dorm. He promised to have the horns delivered to Paul in Brockport, sell them and give the profit to Paul, or drive them back himself when he was going to visit his family in Yonkers in a few months.

Richard was actually kind enough to drive us from Mammoth back to West Thumb, stopping at a general store so we could grab a couple of egg croissant sandwiches, coffee, and orange juices to go.

He made sure we were headed toward Grand Teton National Park on Route 191, shook our hands and drove off back to Mammoth. I reluctantly had to admit to myself that maybe Richard wasn't such a bad guy after all. Like most people he had a lot of good wrapped up in some bad traits, or at least what I considered bad.

Helen

God how I loved the wilderness and remoteness of Wyoming, the rolling green hills leading to white mountain peaks miles away and the sheer vastness of the land stretching as far as I could see. Breathing the clean, crisp air of Wyoming into my lungs was refreshing, a welcome respite from standing on the shoulders of Interstates in New York, Ohio, Illinois, and Kansas.

We were fortunate to get a ride out of West Thumb quickly. A middle-aged couple with German accents, driving a Hertz rental blue 1976 Chevy Impala, stopped at the intersection of Route 191 and 20. They were planning on camping near Jackson Hole, Wyoming and were kind enough to stop at Jenny Lake in Grand Teton National Park on the way there so Paul and I could sightsee. What a beautiful landscape, the clearest blue lake I had ever seen and with the ridiculous steep mountains to the west and I thought, "This is what heaven must be like". We pulled off the main road two other times on the way to Jackson Hole so I could take photographs of buffalo and elk. A two hour non-stop ride took four, but it was worth every minute. The couple dropped us off on the southern edge of Jackson Hole so we wouldn't have to worry about village traffic. Paul and I ate the rest of our gorp, my extra M&M's, and water from our canteens that we had filled up in Jenny Lake.

***

She picked us up outside of Jackson Hole on a late Thursday afternoon when a warm sun was blazing through the blue skies. She was driving a pea green 1969 Plymouth station wagon with two giggly teenage girls riding along.

The girl sitting in the front passenger seat rolled down her window and a voice came from the driver, "Marie, ask them where they're going."

"Los Angeles," Paul said before Marie could speak.

"Well you two have a ways to go, we aren't headed quite that far," said the sultry voiced driver, a forty something year-old looking brunette. Peering in through the passenger side window I could see a woman wearing a tan, floppy, straw hat with a yellow flower sticking out of the brim and dark sunglasses hiding her eyes. Her thin lips were adorned with some shade of red lipstick, elephant shaped earrings swung back and forth from underneath the hat. Draped over her body was a loose fitting sundress with multi-colored spots and pink sandals on her long feet that ended with toenails painted black. Wispy smoke from a Salem cigarette was floating out of the ashtray.

"Let's toss those packs in the back, then you boys can hop in," said the driver.

She got out of the station wagon and opened the rear tailgate so Paul and I could put our packs in. The large, multicolored beads of her necklace jangled around her neck and led my eyes to her breasts, but the bagginess of the dress didn't help satisfy my curiosity.

"Marie, you get in the back seat with Janet, one of you boys up front with me, the other in back with the girls. My name's Helen, like the volcano, Mt. St. Helens," she said. "What's yours?"

"This is Sean, I'm Paul," and he immediately smiled and climbed into the back seat with the girls. Even if they were three or four years younger than us he was going to try and enjoy this ride and make me carry the conversation. Helen got in the driver's seat and I rode shotgun. A jasmine odor wafted through the car from a Little Tree air freshener hanging from the rear view mirror and slightly covered the stench of the cigarette.

Without me asking, Helen began to tell us stories about her life in St. Louis, why she decided to travel in this area for the summer with her daughter Marie and her friend Janet.

"Yeah, my husband of seventeen years decided a few months ago I wasn't young or pretty enough any longer and took off with a twenty-five year old blonde bimbo. I hope she ends up ripping his heart out of his chest like he did with me. Maybe the old fart will have a heart attack when screwing her. At least Marie and I got the house and this station wagon. Don't worry, I'm not really bitter, I think he had been cheating on me for quite a while, probably with more than one young woman, so good riddance. A couple of months later Marie and I decided once school ended we would travel around Montana, Wyoming, and Utah for a couple of weeks. Her father would never travel, at least not with us.

I would have thought a woman traveling with two teenage girls, who picked up two hitchhiking nineteen year old men, would have asked about us, but Helen didn't seem to care much about our story. I think she was harboring feelings from losing her husband and didn't care what we had gone through to get this far. From late August to May Helen was a high school art teacher, which to me explained her attitude and unique flair for fashion. I had always found artsy people a bit...unique.

It was around six p.m. and the sky was already growing faintly dark when we finally pulled into the small, tents only, Station Creek Campground in the Bridger-Teton National Forest. The area was serene and thickly wooded with tall pines. Paul and I pitched our tent, unrolled the sleeping bags inside, and walked a few sites over to see if Helen and the girls needed any help. Obviously they were well-skilled in camping as their large tent was already set up; they had a fire going, and were preparing burgers for the grill. Two empty Pabst Blue Ribbon cans were lying near the car rear door, so Helen seemed ready to enjoy the night and she wasn't sharing any of the ten beers she had left.

The three of them were nice enough to share their meal with us, though, and our contribution was listening to Helen complain about some of her former students as she continued working her way through the twelve-pack of beer. Marie and Janet were content to sit around the campfire and whisper to each other. I think they had heard all of these stories before and just wanted to zone out. We heard some guitar playing from a nearby site and Helen suddenly got up, grabbed a six-pack and told us to join her as she began an unsteady march to the site. The guitar man turned out to be named Ray. He was nice enough to let the five of us sit around his campfire and listen to two Peter, Paul and Mary folk songs he knew the lyrics and chords to. After slamming down a couple more PBR's, Helen began requesting songs that Ray didn't know how to play on the guitar. It got ugly as Helen became obnoxious, loud, and demanding.

"C'mon, surely you know how to play a Dylan, Carole King, or Guthrie song!"

"No, I really don't," said Ray. "I only began playing a few months ago; I'm just trying to enjoy myself a little. Maybe you can sing or play something?"

"That's not the point, I thought you were going to entertain us tonight," said Helen.

I always found it an interesting study in seeing how alcohol affected everyone's personality differently. Some, like Helen, had a meaner side come out, while a lot of guys would become filled with false bravado and want to argue or physically fight. Normally quiet people, like me, might relax their guard and become more social. Helen began criticizing Ray. Maybe she was taking her anger about the divorce out on every man she met, it was hard to tell. But being mean to Ray bothered me almost as much as if she had been tearing me apart. A public humiliation was like having an anchor placed around my neck and just dragged me down, whether it was Ray or me. I had had enough and grabbed one of Helen's beers while she was still bothering Ray and walked back to our tent.

There were shower stalls just a short walk from our tent so I decided this was a good time to be alone and finally get clean again. I hadn't showered in four days, though I did wash myself in the Yellowstone River with my biodegradable soap when Paul and I had been hiking. I grabbed the one bath towel I owned from the bottom of Atlas, my bar of red Lifebuoy soap, and headed to the showers, the starlit night sky and bright crescent moon made the walk enjoyable through the pines. The air temperature was still comfortable and the park was quiet and peaceful. I didn't feel threatened by snakes, bears, raccoons, or other wild animals. Three showers framed by cedar wood were attached together on a cement base with a drain in the middle of each one. The stalls were small, maybe four foot square, at most, with four inches between the door bottom and the cement floor which made it easier to see if one of the stalls was already occupied. All three stalls were empty so I took the one on the left, set my soap on a small rectangular shelf, hung the towel on a hook attached to the door and began undressing. The only place for my clothes seemed to be another hook on the door or just placing them over the door top, which is where I put them. I wasn't wearing much, just cutoff jean shorts, underwear and a white t-shirt. My sandals stayed on my feet; I could only imagine the germs that lurked on the shower floor. The rusted drain cover and spider webs in two of the corners didn't help my queasiness.

I pulled the chain that controlled the water flow and screamed aloud, "Jeezus the water's fuck'n cold!" It felt like a damn glacier river had swept over my body! With my back to the door I let the chain slip from my hand as low groans escaped from my mouth. The water hitting the cement and my outburst must have hidden the creaking of the shower door opening and when I turned around there was Helen gliding in. She hung up her robe and towel and was naked as a jaybird, a PBR in her left hand, faded pink sandals on her feet and a lit cigarette dangling from her smirking skinny red lips.

"Why don't we try conserving the water and share the shower?" Helen coyly suggested.

A real man of the world, studly kind of guy, would have known exactly what to say and do. That wasn't me. I was nineteen, had seen one real, live, naked girl in my life and went into instant shock upon seeing Helen standing there. My mouth dropped open large enough for an apple to fit in, my eyes bugged out like a fly under a microscope, and I stared, transfixed by her boobs gently swaying only a few inches from me.

"What's wrong Sean, you act like you ain't seen a naked lady before," Helen slurred and casually dropped her cigarette on the wet floor, crushing the remaining lit ashes with her sandal.

"Co, co, course I have," I stuttered.

"Yeah, I bet," Helen said. "But don't worry; I'll take care of you."

Helen grabbed my Lifebuoy soap; "oh, I like the nice red color" told me to turn around and began gently rubbing the soap on my shoulders and back as I controlled the shower water flow, which seemed to be getting warmer. She slowly worked her way up and down my wet body.

"How's that feel, Sean?" she asked.

"Nice, the water doesn't seem so cold anymore." I had to give Helen credit; she was great at giving massages.

"I bet. Here, it's your turn to clean me," Helen said, handing me the soap and turning around. So I took turns between running the red bar over her skin and lathering up my hands and rubbing them up and down her legs before she turned around, gave a lustful smile and told me to continue. She didn't have to ask twice.

103

Helen took the lead throughout our rendezvous as we tried several positions in the confined space of the stall before her needs, and mine, were satisfied.

"Alright," she said, finishing her beer and tossing the can over the shower door. "Get your clothes and towel, leave the soap, and get out of here. It's my turn to get clean, and without your help."

Just like that I was sent back to my tent where Paul's snores were sure to keep any raccoons or bears away. I put on my long johns and crawled into my sleeping bag feeling strangely satisfied, yet used. Fortunately sleep came easily.

In the morning I changed into jeans, socks, sneakers and my tie-dye shirt. Paul and I ate a less than thrilling breakfast consisting of the rest of my rye bread and peanut butter as we packed up our belongings. Helen invited us to continue riding with them, which we gladly accepted. It was a beautiful place to camp, but finding another ride so far from any towns would have been extremely difficult. We kept the same seating arrangement; which was a bit awkward for me considering the shower rendezvous, but Helen didn't seem bothered by it at all, though I did notice the sweet smell of Lifebuoy soap remaining on her skin. She had her Rand-McNally road map highlighted in yellow and spread open in the middle of the front seat. Helen appeared to know exactly which route to take on their way to the final stop, at least with us in the car, a four hour drive through Soda Springs and Lava Hot Springs, Idaho then onto Interstate 15 toward Salt Lake City. Paul and I were happy to have such a long ride.

Soon after getting started on state Route 34 we stopped in the tiny town of Alpine, at Charlie's gas station and convenience store, to fill up the car and our growling stomachs.

Charlie's was definitely a small town station, actually one of the few commercial buildings in this tiny town. Charlie himself came out and checked the oil, filled the tank, and cleaned the windshield while we all went inside to shop. Turns out Charlie's wife Betsy worked the counter in the store and did the cooking, so the place was a family affair. The store smelled like fresh fried doughnuts, bacon, and baked muffins. A Husky sitting by the front door raised his head as we walked in, gave a low growl, but otherwise didn't seem to take much notice of us.

Helen, of course, gravitated immediately to the beer cooler so she could restock with a twelve-pack of Schlitz. Marie and Janet bought a dozen doughnuts, three small orange juice bottles, two Dr. Peppers, and a Fanta. I think they wanted to make sure Mom had something in her body besides beer. Paul bought the largest coffee I had ever seen, which must have been at least 20 ounces, then he poured two creamers and three sugar packets in it. He also picked up two Hostess apple pies, a Jack Link's beef jerky stick, a peppermint gum package, two apples, a banana, and a postcard with a jackalope on it.

"Who are you writing to Paul?" I asked.

"My parents, of course, I brought a few stamps, why don't you send a card out, Sean?" he said. "It'll only take a few days to get there and maybe let them know you're okay."

"Yeah, that's probably not a bad idea," I replied.

I chose a card that pictured Grand Teton National Park and wrote:

Hello from Wyoming. Paul and I are having a great time and have met several nice people along the way. The Millers treated us like family in Colorado, loved their indoor swimming pool! We are on our way to Salt Lake City and then out to California. The weather has been great. Hope you two are doing well.

Love, Sean

In addition to the card I bought two rolls of Kodachrome film and the smallest coffee Charlie's offered, eight ounces of strong black mud, or so it seemed. Maybe it wasn't the freshest pot of coffee ever made. This was one time I found it necessary to add cream to the cup so it was palatable. I never drank coffee before this trip but suddenly found it a great energizer. I also picked up two Butterfingers, a home baked cinnamon roll the size of my hand, a Styrofoam container of hot bacon slices (it's impossible to smell bacon and not want to eat a few slices) and orange juice. I grabbed a box of Ritz and graham crackers, a jar of Peter Pan peanut butter, and two cans of tuna fish and placed them in Atlas. Betsy kindly let Paul and I refill our canteens from her sink. In a rare moment of goodwill I paid the nine dollar gasoline bill, figuring it was the least I could do for Helen taking us on such a long ride (and the unmentioned shower adventure). Charlie let us mail our postcards from the station. I hoped it wasn't the Pony Express taking the cards back East. I gave the Husky a slice of bacon on the way back to the wagon.

The drive from Alpine through Soda Springs and on past Lava Hot springs was uneventful. We all concentrated on our food, sharing the doughnuts (the coconut covered doughnut was my favorite, but the lemon filled one was a close second) and sipping coffee and juice, though I ended up tossing most of my coffee/mud out the window. The scenery was spectacular to an East coast teenager who was used to flat lands. I had hiked plenty of "mountains" in the east, but 4,000 feet was just a bump in the road out here. At every intersection or four wheel drive path I saw go out from the main highway I wondered who lived there and if they realized how lucky they were? I wanted to explore every road. The promise of discoveries along each road, whether dirt, stone, or paved was difficult to resist. The country was so big and I was an inconsequential tiny piece of it and desperately wanted to see everything.

After a couple of hours we merged onto Interstate 15 and headed south toward Salt Lake City. As we went along there were dozens of oil refineries, stacks with light smoke spilling into the air, oil rigs jutting out of the ground, it was really striking and quite different scenery than the mountains of Wyoming or Colorado.

Helen kept saying over and over, "who did this, this is terrible, and why would anyone destroy the land like this?" I actually found her statements annoying.

It took all of my restraint not to say, "We did you stupid idiot! You're driving this huge station wagon around the country, how do you think we get the fuel? You think it's fucking magic?" But I kept all the yelling in my head, no need to get tossed onto the side of the road now. I just let Helen keep on ranting every time she saw a new refinery area. At least she wasn't drinking her Schlitz beer while driving, only chain smoking Salems. After several hours we finally reached the heart of Salt Lake City. Helen dropped Paul and I off at the exit to the Mormon Temple in downtown Salt Lake so we could walk over to the on-ramp and continue on I-15. We said goodbye to Marie and Janet, Helen seemed preoccupied with moving on with their trip. Once Paul and I grabbed our backpacks she gave a small wave, blew a kiss, and drove off, taking my Lifebuoy soap with her.

Michael McCullough

Speed Buggy

It was bittersweet losing Helen driving us across Idaho and a chunk of Utah, while also enjoying the company of Marie and Janet, but she obviously had her own agenda and we had ours. That type of ride and meeting of diverse people is what we signed up for when beginning our trek. Except for the transportation method, I thought of us as modern day Bilbo Baggins and Dwalin. Bilbo would be me, surprisingly adventurous and brave, in a quiet sort of way. Unfortunately I didn't have a magic ring that would let me disappear or a dagger that would warn of dangerous people. There certainly were many times in my life those would have been nice options to have. Paul was strong, loyal, stubborn, and a fighter, similar to Dwalin. We never knew who would pick us up, how far they would take us, or what kind of person they would be. Every time we stood on the shoulder of a road, held our sign, and stuck out our thumbs, we took a chance.

Left at the on-ramp to Interstate 15, we didn't have the opportunity to get supplies to make a new sign, SOUTH, so we stuck out our thumbs, stood next to our packs, and hoped for the best. It was a slow go, nobody seemed willing to give two guys a ride on this Friday afternoon. I was beginning to think Utah people didn't like hitchhikers, or maybe it was against the prevailing religion, the Mormon faith. At least the weather was decent and we weren't getting drenched by any rain, only more tanned from the Utah sun. I was listening to a local AM station play the Kinks, "Lazing on a Sunny Afternoon in the Summertime," when finally, around five-thirty, a teal colored 1972 Ford Maverick stopped. The twenty-something year old, straight blonde haired, male driver, dressed in a gold and red Burger King uniform, yelled out the open passenger side window, "Hey, get in guys, I can give you a ride. How far are you going?"

"Eventually to California," said Paul.

"Hah, well I'm sure not going that far. I just wanted some company for the ride home from work." He lit an Old Gold cigarette and turned down the Foghat song playing on the radio. I got in the back seat and Paul rode shotgun. The Maverick smelled like a combination of smoke and French fry grease. Several crunched up empty Burger King bags were on the floor near me. At least the driver liked the food he cooked, though he was so skinny I'm not sure where the Whoppers and fries went in his body. There didn't appear to be a fat cell on him or much muscle either. He must have burned all the calories while working over the fryers.

"I'm a shift manager at a BK in Salt Lake, my name is Warren," which I already knew since his name tag was still pinned to his shirt. "What do they call you two?"

"Well, I'm Paul and that putz in the back is called Sean. How far can you take us this afternoon?"

"I get off the expressway at Spanish Fork, about an hour away. Sorry it couldn't be further."

"We'll take anything we can get, every ride helps, thanks for stopping."

"No problem, I did a lot of hitchhiking myself as a teenager."

Warren, like a lot of the people who picked us up, wanted to talk about his life, which was fine with me. What a great way to learn about people and different parts of the country. They were doing us a favor by giving us rides, so why not sit back and listen?

"I know you guys probably don't think much of someone like me whose job is just working at Burger King, but I'm doing okay, ya know? I'm twenty-seven, worked my way up from the French fry guy to assistant manager, so I'm happy. There's a new BK opening soon in Provo, a lot closer to my home in Mapleton, and the district manager promised me a manager position. For now I'm just going to try and climb the ladder, see if I can get to district manager, maybe higher up, who knows. My girlfriend is a hair stylist, together we're doing okay."

"Hey, I'm in college and have no idea what I'm going to do after graduating, who knows if I'll make it through four years, you're doing fine, have a plan, I've got nothing laid out, just kind of going through the motions right now, taking what comes," I said.

"Besides, being in charge, a boss, taking responsibility for a restaurant, those are skills a lot of companies would want," added Paul.

Too soon Warren exited the Interstate, let us out of the car, and said,

"If you're ever in this area again, check out a Burger King, you never know, it might be my restaurant."

"Absolutely, we will do that," said Paul.

We waved as he turned left toward state Route 6. My stomach was growling from not eating for hours and smelling the food remnants inside of Warren's Maverick. We walked over to the on-ramp hoping for a ride so we could continue south on I-15, it was after seven p.m. and daylight was quickly fading. There was more standing or sitting on the guardrail under the streetlights watching cars, pickups, motorcycles, and semi's turn onto the ramp, speed up and drive off into the Utah night. I ate a sleeve of graham crackers while Paul finished off his beef jerky. Two hours later we were still standing in the same spot. I needed Warren's Burger King food.

"Let's get up on the Interstate, Sean, this is ridiculous and not a place I want to spend the night."

"Fine by me."

We walked up the ramp and stood under a streetlight on I-15, not too far from the ramp so that drivers could see us on the highway. Thirty minutes later a Utah State Police officer turned on his flashing lights and pulled in front of us with his headlights blasting our eyes.

"Not again," I sighed. I could see the cop had a high and tight Marine Corps style cut before he put his hat on, a hand on his pistol, and a pissed off look on his pock-marked face. He looked to be in his thirties, around my height but thirty pounds heavier. I had a bad feeling about this.

"What are you two doing out here!" he demanded as he strode up toward us.

"We're trying to get a ride, heading to California," said Paul. One would think our backpacks would give legitimacy to our quest, but this cop wasn't having it.

"Being a pedestrian on the Interstate is dangerous for you and drivers, oh, and by the way, against the law," added the Officer. He certainly didn't have the demeanor of Sheriff Andy Taylor or even

Officer Quinn from Kansas. He reminded me of a drill sergeant, maybe that's why he still had the crew cut. I could see from his nametag he was Officer Mahoney, who was obviously full of himself and supposed power. I didn't have the feeling this was going to end well for Paul and me.

"Give me your ID's, you both are getting at least one ticket for being vagrants and maybe more. I could decide to throw you in jail, how does that sound?"

It sounded fucking stupid and overblown to me. Throw us in jail, go ahead you fucking moron, at least I'd get a warm bed, an indoor bathroom, and breakfast in the morning. Vagrants? Fuck you. I'm trying to get the fuck out of this place, not be a bum here. Wouldn't it be better to let us continue on our way and get out of Spanish Fork, maybe just give a warning and tell us to get back to the on-ramp? Of course that conversation was all in my head but it sure was tempting to spit out.

"New York, huh, think you are something special coming from New York City?"

"You can see from the licenses we live in Brockport, it's about six hours from New York City and in the middle of farmland. So no, we don't think we are so special, only a couple of college guys taking a summer trip," I growled.

In my head again I was thinking; what moron thought six million people living in New York City were special? Maybe some of them were, but not everyone, maybe parts of the City were special, but not all of it. What a dumb ass. My response didn't make him happy, it only made Officer Dipshit spit on the ground in disgust.

"Here's your tickets for being vagrants, if you are still anywhere around here in another hour, especially near the Interstate, it'll be jail time for you two," warned Officer Mahoney.

"Yes sir," said Paul, being overly polite. "We'll just go back down to the ramp and hope for a ride soon."

What happened to the tough guy who got a drunk and disorderly citation with me back in Brockport?

Fuck you, I said in my head again. I think he was secretly jealous of my long, curly brown hair, maybe he was having a bad night, or his wife had just left him, or he was just a big, mean, bully. Maybe in high school kids used to steal his lunches and now Officer Mahoney was using his badge to get back at people. It was kind of funny, at one time I thought of going to a community college for criminal justice, now this jackhat was making me glad I didn't if this was the typical cop attitude.

With that fun conversation over Paul and I went to the entrance of the on-ramp. By the blessings of the gods a light green 1970 Ford Country Squire station wagon stopped next to us just twenty minutes later and a forty-something year old man asked if we needed a ride. There was no hesitation on our part, we were willing to take a chance just to get away from Officer Dipshit; I mean Mahoney. He drove us to Scipio, Utah, only a bit over an hour away, but at least we didn't have to worry about being thrown in jail anymore.

***

buckle up tight boys
take a magic carpet ride
through the desert air

At a Big Boy restaurant near the exit Paul and I each ordered a super Big Boy burger, fries and a Coke to go. We were starving and health food be damned. Standing outside eating our burgers wondering what the next move would be, a kelly green 1972 Plymouth Road Runner pulled up in the parking spot next to us, breaking the silence of the night sky. It seemed like the entire car was shaking until the motor was turned off, it might have continued shaking for a few minutes after that. The driver, who appeared to be in his late twenties, with long straight brown hair parted in the middle, got out of the car. He was wearing a green O'Reilly Auto Parts worker's shirt and blue jeans. He kept wringing his hands together, glanced in our direction, and walked quickly to the restaurant, looking like he was on drugs, running from someone, or really had to pee.

After almost swallowing my burger whole to calm my growling stomach, I began dipping the greasy, salty fries in ketchup, savoring each bite, when the Road Runner driver came out holding a bag of food and a drink cup. He glanced over at us and said, "You need a ride?"

It was late, almost one a.m., and thanks to Officer Dipshit it had been an especially difficult day.

"Absolutely," I said. "We're heading to the Pacific Ocean, how far can you take us?"

"Interesting," said the Road Runner man. "I'm going to the Los Angeles area as quickly as possible and need to stay awake for the night while I drive, want to join me?"

"Yeah, sounds great," I said, maybe a bit too soon before knowing what we were getting into.

"Throw your packs in the trunk and get strapped in," said the Road Runner man. We were in an area of the country that looked like a desert and it was late. Our two options were to sleep out in the grass next to the Interstate again, with lizards or other species of animals I didn't care to be around, or ride with this guy. Paul and I got in the car, he was in the front seat and I sat in the middle of the rear seat.

"Oh, I'm Cliff, what are your names?"

"I'm Paul, that's Sean."

When Cliff started the ignition the car engine was so loud I could barely hear what was being said in the front seat. Gravel was flying from the rear tires as we left the parking lot and got on I-15. Cliff pressed the accelerator, the Road Runner began shaking, and I was sure the engine was going to fall out and we would all die out here, our bodies strewn across the highway being picked apart by vultures before anyone found us. We were in a full-size Crashmobile. I cinched the seat belt tighter against my waist.

"Don't worry about the car, guys, I replaced the engine yesterday and it may need to be broken in. I'm sure in a few miles it'll quiet down," yelled Cliff over the noise.

Never was a statement so untrue. A few minutes later we were traveling at ninety miles per hour. The Angel of Death was riding on the roof as we passed cars in the left or right lanes of the Interstate. Apparently trying to stay in one lane didn't seem to make sense to Cliff. In a way we were blessed that at this hour of the night traffic was thin.

"My girl broke up with me and I may or may not have punched out her brother back in Salt Lake. She left for Thousand Oaks, near L.A., possibly to live with her aunt, and I'm going to find her and get her back," said Cliff.

"Well, I guess that makes sense, but do we have to get there so quickly, what if you get a speeding ticket?" I yelled from the backseat. The Big Boy fries weren't sitting in my stomach so well anymore.

"I'm not worried," said Cliff.

Coincidentally enough, an hour later we got pulled over by a Utah state police officer, fortunately it wasn't Officer Mahoney. Cliff's ticket was for driving thirty mph over the limit. When the cop finally let us go Cliff said, "Open the glove box and shove the ticket in there." Paul did as he was told and found a pile of other speeding tickets already in the glove box.

"Told you I didn't care about another ticket," said Cliff.

Neither Paul nor I could sleep all night. Between speeding along at eighty to ninety miles an hour in the dark and also feeling like the engine wasn't connected to the frame, it was impossible to relax. We entered Las Vegas near dawn and stopped at a Waffle House off of I-15 for breakfast. My stomach was in such turmoil from the ride it was all I could do to eat a waffle and have a couple of cups of coffee to help keep me awake. I had sweat through my tie-dye shirt from being so nervous about Cliff's driving and changed into my 'keep on truckin' shirt'. Cliff seemed to not want Paul and I to have any time alone to discuss the options in front of us, like staying in Vegas for a night or two. We played and lost at the slot machines in the restaurant and got back in the shaking Road Runner. Continuing on with Cliff made no sense other than being worried about getting a ride across the desert and wanting to get to the Pacific Ocean. We could have easily stayed in a cheap motel, walked to the nicer casinos and tried to get a ride later. Separately we came to the decision to take what was being offered now, another stupid move on our parts. How often would we have the chance to party in Vegas? What a couple of idiots, so concerned about rides and time, like we didn't have all summer if we wanted it. We weren't on any particular schedule and could have easily wasted a few days along the Strip.

Leaving Vegas Cliff wasn't any more careful with speeding. He received another ticket near Baker, California and had Paul add it to the glove box collection. We arrived in Oxnard, a bit north of Los Angeles, before noon and were unceremoniously left at the intersection of Routes 101 and 126.

"I'm so glad to be out of that death trap of a car," said Paul.

"Yeah, that was a long, fast trip, over six hundred miles, but I don't think I'd want to repeat it. My body still feels like it's shaking as much as the car was. I've never held onto a door handle so tight or for so long before. I hope his girlfriend is happy to see him, but I have a feeling it wasn't a nice parting of the ways," I said.

It was eighty degrees, sunny, not a cloud in the sky. No wonder people loved California living. Now it was time to head to one of our main destinations on this crazy trip, Big Sur.

Big Sur

cold beer, salty air
oaks, mountains, canyon, river
steep cliffs, crashing waves

One of our shortest ever wait times for a ride happened after being left in Oxnard by Cliff. Fifteen minutes after he dropped us off, a 1970 canary yellow VW camper van with a bouquet of flowers painted on the rear passenger side, and a white roof, stopped at the red light near the intersection. The outside of the van was impeccably clean, like it had just come out of a car wash.

The male passenger yelled, "Where are you heading to?"

"Big Sur!" Paul yelled back. The traffic noise was intense.

"Well, get in, Patrick and I are going up 101 and Route 1 to Monterey, Big Sur is right on the way, you don't smoke right?" he said at the same time the sliding side door was opening.

"Not cigars or cigarettes, no," I said.

"Good, you can get in, my name is Joshua."

The light had turned green and car horns started blaring behind the van. Paul and I looked at each other, shrugged our shoulders and got in. This couldn't be a worse ride than Road Runner man and they were taking us right to our destination. There was plenty of space on the floor for our packs and a bench seat for us. This VW already seemed safer and calmer than the criminals we had met in Kansas. There was a vanilla smell wafting through the van. A James Taylor eight track was playing "You've Got a Friend." I heard a small bell and suddenly a miniature, curly, white furry poodle crawled out from under our seat.

"Oh, don't mind Celeste, she's a bit curious about who's joining us in the van," said Joshua. With that Celeste jumped onto Paul's lap and began licking his face before settling down for a rest.

Patrick looked back at us and said, "You guys look hungry, have a couple of Joshua's homemade chocolate chip cookies," and handed me a tin filled with cookies.

"Do you want to share your names?" asked Joshua, as I greedily took a bite of a cookie.

"Yeah, absolutely, these cookies are delicious, thanks for sharing, I'm Sean and that's Paul stuffing his mouth with a cookie. Should we let Celeste eat one?"

"No, here's a Milk-Bone she can chew on. Paul, put her down on the floor so Celeste won't leave crumbs on your shorts. Where did you begin hitchhiking?" asked Patrick.

"Upstate New York," replied Paul after he finished chewing.

"Whoa, that's a long way, how long have you been gone?"

"We left on June 27, but stayed in Yellowstone for a few days."

"Nice. You must have had some long rides. Well, relax and enjoy this one, if we don't stop it'll be about four and a half hours. We've done this trip so many times and the views seem to get better each time," said Joshua.

Seeing the coastline, the mountains, driving along the curvy road on this sunny California day was fantastic. I would have been happy stopping anywhere on this road to camp and spend a few days. I was exhausted from the overnight ride in the shaky Road Runner, but had no problem staying awake on this part of our adventure. It was easy to sit back, relax, and enjoy the ride. We passed through Santa Barbara, Pismo Beach, Morro Beach, and San Simeon. The music coming from the 8-track player continued with Carly Simon, Carole King, Joni Mitchell, and Donovan. There were speakers in four corners of the van and a makeshift bed was behind our seat.

On the way to Big Sur Paul made the four of us stop at a local farm and pick blueberries. Fortunately for Paul, Joshua and Patrick seemed to be excited about taking fresh blueberries to their friends in Monterey. They were friendly, kind, just the kind of people in my naive mind I expected to meet in California. They dropped us off near the entrance to Julia Pfeiffer Burns State Park and continued on to Monterey. It was cooler here; much different than Oxnard. I felt a bit strange carrying pints of berries as Paul and I walked up to the campground kiosk to check in. Big Sur was not the California of my imagination. Where were the beaches covered with sun-screened bikini clad girls surfing, or laying on beach towels, and just waiting for guys like Paul and I to hit on them?

I thought the campground would be something really special, with tent sites near the ocean and a gentle breeze wafting through cooling our bodies. Nope, no it wasn't. The campground was a hike in from the road with a small area for cars to park. Tents were strewn in little more than a field with a few trees here and there. A couple of outhouses were the only facilities available; there were no showers or real bathrooms. This was a rustic campground, but still better than trying to sleep on the side of an Interstate.

Paul and I found a spot near a tree that provided some shade and set up our small, green tent. He immediately befriended a couple that was headed to a general store and got us a ride. Beer, that was our main concern, a couple of six-packs of nice cold beer. It had been a long, anxiety laden trip through Utah and much of California, with no sleep, and we needed alcohol.

When we got to the checkout counter with our two bags of Wise Ridgies potato chips, a twelve pack of Liberty Ale, a loaf of Boudin sourdough bread, a jar of Peter Pan peanut butter, a jar of Welch's strawberry jelly, and a bag of Reese's Peanut Butter cups, the clerk asked for ID, which we happily provided. Both of us were nineteen, so no concern about buying alcohol, right? Wrong. Who knew you had to be twenty-one to drink in California? We'd been drinking legally since eighteen in New York but now weren't allowed? It seemed ridiculous, but the clerk was not going to let us slide by. Fortunately our new found campground friends were old enough, took the beer and our money and made us wait outside the store as they bought the most important ingredient of our dinner.

Back at the tent site I was starving as Paul and I slapped together a few peanut butter and jelly sandwiches on sourdough bread. We hadn't had a real meal since the Waffle House in Vegas, more than twelve hours ago. Thankfully I could live on good hearty bread, peanut butter, water, and beer.

"Eat some blueberries, too," Paul said. "Try something fresh and healthy for your body for a change."

"I don't even like blueberries, they're too squishy, but maybe with a beer they'll be okay," I said. "I'll probably be pooping blue tomorrow. Man you're crazy with this healthy food crap. Give it to me out of box or can then I'll know it's healthy. Next you'll be shoving yogurt down my throat."

"Oh yeah, blueberries and yogurt, that would have been a great side dish. You should have suggested that when we were at the store."

"Eww, no, yuck, yogurt smells like curdled milk, it makes me want to vomit. I'm glad you forgot to buy some."

After our gourmet dinner, including a few ales apiece, it began to get cooler from the ocean breeze and the sun going down, so I changed into jeans, a t-shirt, flannel shirt and sneakers before we headed over to a large campfire with a dozen or so people around it. I was a bit apprehensive about intruding, but followed the extrovert Paul. Several joints were being passed around so they seemed like our kind of people and didn't mind at all having us join them. Of course there was a guitar player, and the next thing I knew Paul was strumming on the thing and began singing Pete Seeger's "If I Had a Hammer." He followed it up with his own version of "Gorilla" by James Taylor. When he finished we all clapped and I got jarred out of my drunken stupor by a Peter Fonda look-a-like who just couldn't let me be.

"Sean, right, that's your name?"

"Yeah."

"Well, what's your talent? You must be able to do something like your friend here? Can you sing? I'm guessing not since you've barely said four words since being here."

"Sometimes I find it nice to be an observer of human interactions, but you are correct, I have no discernable talents. I dance like a moose, can't sing worth a lick, and play guitar like I'm picking ticks from a farmyard mutt, but, well, I can hit hard."

"Hit, you like to hit people? You feel like hitting me now?"

"No, of course not," I said. Really I kind of did, I just wanted to be left alone, but I was too stoned to stand up steady on my feet, much less throw a punch. My eyeballs were spinning inside the sockets. Instead I took another toke, passed it on, and had a gulp of beer.

"What if I tell a story instead?"

"Go ahead, I'm listening," said phony Peter Fonda.

"There is nothing like the smell of grass in late August, when high school football practice is in full swing. Imagine it's the second week of two-a-day practices, a hot, humid Tuesday night and Bobbie Jackson; our two-hundred twenty pound muscle bound fullback has burst through the defensive line with only you, a six-foot one inch, one-hundred sixty pound outside linebacker between him and the goal line. Bobbie doesn't believe in dancing around defenders, he finds joy directly hitting them, to see who has the most guts and can stand up to him. He uses his human rhinoceros body to test you and discover if you are going to flinch ever so slightly to avoid a full-frontage direct hit. Bobbie lived for those kinds of moments, didn't matter if it was a real game or just a late summer scrimmage with teammates.

In less than a second you have to decide, are you going to take him on or move to the side and make a pretend tackle? Instinctively I react, getting into a tackling position that has been drilled into me for four years now. Sweat is pouring down my face, my arms go wide, up on my toes, moving, quick feet, and Bobbie is going down. My face mask hit Bobbie square in his abdomen, face up; I swear I could see his six-pack abs through the dirty, sweat-stained practice jersey. My arms circled around his body as I began to lift him up and throw him to the ground.

No, no, it wasn't me lifting him, he was lifting me with his forearms, tossing me into the air like a rag doll and I was flying backwards. As I lay on the ground pulling the August grass out of my helmet once again, watching Bobbie run to the end zone, I knew this smell would stay embedded in my brain forever. I suppose I gained some measure of respect from the coaches and teammates for standing my ground, but wrapping the human rhino up would have been so much sweeter."

"Not a bad story, Sean," said phony Peter Fonda. "Have another toke."

Which I did.

The next thing I remember a potato bug was crawling on my cheek heading for my left nostril. I reached out with my right hand and flung it across the burnt grass where he landed rolled up in a tight little ball. Unhurt and unfazed by the flight he teetered away looking for more food. My eyes began watering from the early morning sun. I struggled to get my vision and tried to remember why I wasn't in the tent, but in a field with Atlas for a pillow. Suddenly the feeling of having to pee flooded over me. Not just pee, but whiz a stream that could flood any tents that were within twenty feet of my sleeping bag. GET ME OUT OF THIS THING! Damn this zipper. Christ I have to go! Please God, just this once, if you let me out and run to the port-a-john without pissing my shorts I promise I'll be good. Really, this time I will be. Why did I zip this bag all the way up to the top? Oh, yeah, snakes, so scared one would crawl in with me during the night to stay warm. I hate snakes, I hated them in Wyoming and I still hated them, who knew if Big Sur had snakes, I wasn't taking any chances.

Urghh, maybe if I just roll a bit the zipper will loosen. Oh crap, I just rolled into a box of …what the hell, blueberries? No wonder the potato bug was on my face. What a fucking great morning this is. After a few more seconds of flaying around I got the zipper down and was free! Look at me, same shorts as last night at the campfire, same shirt, bare feet, oh well, just run dammit, I have to go so bad. If anyone is in the port-a-john I'm peeing right next to it. I can't hold it any longer.

Empty stall, empty bladder. Sweet Jesus that felt good. Thank you God, I'll be good for as long as I can be, at least for today. You won't regret this. Man, I drank too many beers last night. And Peter Fonda, yeah, he started giving me shots of Tequila, which may have been a mistake. I don't even like Tequila; I hope I didn't eat the worm at the bottom of the bottle.

Where is Paul? Where is the tent? It seems like every tent in here is a green Coleman like ours. I staggered to my backpack, and standing there shivering due to a cool ocean breeze, briefly naked in the middle of the campground, changed into clean underwear, jeans, socks, hiking boots, my flannel shirt and baseball hat. California was supposed to be hot, sunny, white sandy beaches, surfboards, and girls, lots of girls lying around on towels, strutting up and down the beach, and waiting for me to rub suntan lotion on them. But, no, not this Big Sur campground. I grabbed my journal and a pen and finally located the green tent. I could see a couple of empty blueberry pints next to it.

I walked over and heard Paul snoring and began to unzip the tent flap until I saw four feet instead of two sticking out from the open sleeping bag. The lucky bastard. No wonder I was sleeping in the field. Crap, now what will I eat for breakfast? All of our food, except some blueberries, was in the tent. No way was I eating any more blueberries. Fortunately two beers had been left next to the tent, which I immediately grabbed even if they were slightly warm, and walked to the nearest tree I could climb. Tan Oak, isn't that what the Park Ranger said last night? I remembered staggering around the campground after leaving the campfire, seeing the Ranger and thinking, "Uh oh, now I'm in trouble. It's going to be like Officer Mahoney all over again."

Underage drinking, holding a beer, high as a kite and the Ranger says, "A little party going on inside your head, huh?"

"Yes, yes sir, a bit."

"Well don't overdo it son."

"Ththanks, I won't sir, I'll be okay."

"Tan Oak."

I just stared at him. "Your other beer man, you set it by that Tan Oak tree."

"Oh, yeah, I see it now, thank you."

The Ranger watched as I tried my best to walk in a straight line to the tree and my beer. I picked the bottle up, raised it to toast him, and he waved and continued down the path toward some other late night partiers.

And that's how I knew the tree I was climbing was a Tan Oak. I climbed about ten feet up, found a nice limb to sit on, had a great view of the campground, and could just make out the ocean in the distance. I pulled out my beer breakfast, not quite Rice Krispies, but it temporarily satisfied my hunger pains and somehow began to clear the cobwebs from my brain. I balanced the beer between my legs and began to write in my journal.

Once Paul and his companion woke up and got themselves clean we went exploring. We located the Partington trail and took the north section to a rocky beach and the Pacific Ocean. Wanting to embrace the entire experience at Big Sur we came back to take the path to a cove, which required a sixty foot hike through a tunnel carved through the rock that was built in the 1880s to transport trees to ships anchored nearby. The area may not have had the dozens of bikini clad women I was hoping to see, but was a beautiful place to visit. It was a peaceful natural setting, not crowded, and quiet, except for the sound of robins, swallows, finches, or the occasional woodpecker, among other bird species.

The rest of Sunday was spent relaxing by a campfire with Paul, myself, his new friend, who it turned out was named Melanie, her traveling companion, and a couple of other campers. It was a good night with quiet conversations, a few shared joints, hot dogs cooked over the coals, with blueberries, potato chips, and peanut butter cups as side dishes. Melanie's tent mate decided to sleep in the backseat of their car rather than intrude on their private time or join me in my two person tent, which I had no problem with. She was average in looks, which didn't bother me at all, but really nasty when speaking to me, like I wasn't worthy of making conversation with. I was pretty sure she didn't know how to smile. I felt like she had a black heart, just looking for the bad in everything and everybody. Who needed to be around such a negative person? Not me. It was nice to enjoy the privacy of my little green tent with no potato bugs crawling on my body. I could write in my journal using a flashlight, stretch out, enjoy the space, and not worry about getting trapped in my sleeping bag.

Hells Angels

Monday morning, July 12, Paul and I were back on Highway 101 hoping for another ride. The day began a bit cool, which seemed to be typical Big Sur weather. Apparently I was destined to never be at the warm, white sand, California beaches. Instead Paul and I wore jeans, boots, and I had a tie dye t-shirt underneath my well-worn flannel shirt, while Paul wore his green and gold Brockport State Football sweatshirt. Paul had exchanged phone numbers with Melanie before we hit the road, but from his past history I was pretty sure there would be no future contact. For breakfast we finished off our sourdough bread and peanut butter. I was listening to Three Dog Night, "Easy to be Hard" on KAZU-AM from Monterey on my transistor radio when it began to rain, a fine mist accompanying the fog rolling in from the ocean. We dug our bright yellow ponchos from our packs and hoped someone would take pity and give us a ride soon. Paul had made a new sign, "Seattle" which we took turns holding, before tiring and propping it against Atlas and watching the ink slowly run off.

Four long, soggy hours later our time on the road was finally rewarded when a light gold-colored 1973 Mercury Capri quickly swerved onto the skinny roadside shoulder. Paul and I ran up to the car and saw a scrawny looking, brown-bearded man wearing a Harley-Davidson cap and a black leather jacket in the driver's seat, and an angelic faced, long, brown haired, pony-tailed woman wearing a white blouse with a tan vest over it and a multi-colored beaded necklace, sitting in the passenger seat.

We anticipated the usual question, "where you heading to?" asked the man, leaning over the woman and out the passenger side window. I guess the sign with a big "Seattle" on it wasn't obvious enough, but in his defense the letters were a little smudged from the rain.

Paul answered, "We're going to Seattle to see my grandparents. We came from Upstate New York, made it to the ocean like we wanted, and now need to head north."

"It's late in the day and you two look a bit wet," said the bearded man. "We can take you up to Oakland and tomorrow you can continue from there, okay? We have room for you to stay in our townhouse in the city, if you want. You can eat, shower, and sleep in a dry space. My name is Alan; this is my wife, Yvonne. You two are called?"

"Paul."

"Sean."

"Sean, a good Irish name," said Alan. Yvonne, for her part, was quietly listening to the conversation and humming to the radio playing, "Monday, Monday."

"Getting out of the fog and mist and staying with you two sounds like a great idea, thanks," I said.

Alan walked with a slight limp as he got out of the car and opened the trunk so we could put our packs and wet ponchos in it before climbing into the backseat. These two didn't know us and already offered us a dry place to stay? I felt lucky but apprehensive at the same time.

"What are your zodiac signs?" asked Alan. That seemed a strange way to begin our ride to Oakland, but I had read a few books on astrology so...what the heck. It was interesting how my personality generally matched up to my sign, not that I believed it all, but fascinating nonetheless.

"Scorpio," I said. "I was born on Thanksgiving Day, November 22, my father stayed at work to earn holiday pay while my mother gave birth to me. It was the only way for him to be able to pay the hospital bill."

"Did you know your spirit animal is an African elephant? They have long memories, just like Scorpios. Make a Scorpio mad and they will never forget it."

"Hah," laughed Paul. "He definitely clomps around a basketball court like an elephant, can jump about as high as one too."

"Screw you Paul, I can jump higher than you, you fat bastard!"

"Anyhow," continued Alan. "I bet you are really emotional and intense and have to always be moving to feel alive, right?" said Alan.

126

"So far it sounds like me, I absolutely need to be active. My life is always about staying in motion; playing sports, hiking, whatever. I'm guessing you're a Scorpio too, that's how you know all this stuff?"

"Yes, I am, but I learned about all of the signs. Let's see, what else can I tell you about yourself? You're protective and loyal to people you love, you're empathetic, and probably feel like you're absorbing the feelings that other people are having. Most Scorpios can read a room quickly and clue into how everyone else is feeling."

"What's your sign, Paul?" asked Yvonne.

"Virgo," answered Paul. "I was born in September."

"Oh, so do you think you have the typical Virgo traits?"

"I'm not sure, I've never really looked into it too much, it's just a bunch of hogwash to me," said Paul.

"Well, are you hard-working, reliable, stubborn, and honest? Maybe you're a bit of a skeptic, sarcastic, and always striving for perfection?"

In my head I'm thinking, jeez, these two sound like they memorized or wrote a book on astrology.

"It's possible I'm some of those, I guess you'll find out more about me as the day goes on," said Paul. I think Paul was bored by the entire conversation and was pretending to listen to be polite.

"Oh, he's definitely stubborn, don't worry about that, and sarcastic too," I said.

Two and a half hours later we parked on a street in downtown Oakland that was lined with skinny, attached, brick townhomes with equally small front porches. Once inside Yvonne let us toss our clothes that hadn't been cleaned since Yellowstone into their washer, then occupied herself in the kitchen with cooking spaghetti for dinner. Paul and I stayed in the living room with Alan and an old, calm, German Shepherd named, "Admiral" who seemed to be content laying in the corner on a well-loved dog bed.

"Admiral doesn't seem to mind us being here at all, is he supposed to offer you protection?" I asked.

"Well, he used to, we all get old and tired, Admiral has too, I guess. He's earned the right to be lazy as far as Yvonne and I am concerned." Alan continued on his astrology kick, "You know, Sean, being Scorpio, you have a lot of strength, you need to learn how to use it. Being loyal, honest, and intense you can accomplish a lot in life. Don't let my size fool you. I'm a member of the Hells Angels, though I participate in less activities than I used to, ever since my accident and with Yvonne coming into my life. Does that bother or scare you two?"

"No, well maybe a bit, it's not like they've had a lot of positive press over the years," I said.

Yvonne came out carrying a tray with three mugs of Anchor beer, a plate of assorted cheeses, pepperoncinis, and crackers. I felt like I was in a friendly restaurant, but Yvonne didn't seem to mind being alone in the kitchen. I could hear her softly singing Carole King songs while she cooked.

"I still have my Harley, of course, it's the only vehicle allowed in our garage."

"Why did you stop hanging with the Angels all the time?" asked Paul.

"Being an Angel can be an adrenaline rush, I love being part of the group. The sense of brotherhood, riding together, caring for each other, there's nothing like it. But after a few high profile public disturbances, the misunderstanding of our role at various events, and being arrested myself several times for driving while intoxicated, speeding tickets and a few other things, it seemed I should take things a little slower or I'd probably die an early death. I had turned forty and around the same time met Yvonne, who was a receptionist at the physical therapist's office I was going to after my latest motorcycle crash. She finally accepted a date with me after I kept going in for every session with fresh flowers for her. The crash is why I walk with a limp. She changed my life, but understands I'm a member forever and doesn't even think of saying I need to sell the Harley. Actually we take rides on it most weekends, join up with other members of the local Club and have a great time. I'm the head mechanic at a local motorcycle shop and work on all types of bikes, but Harleys will always have a special place in my heart. Yvonne, the Hells Angels, and motorcycles are my life, and Admiral, of course, can't forget him."

Alan continued, "After dating for a couple of months I discovered Yvonne is the most wonderful singer I've ever heard. It took a long time for her to feel comfortable singing for me, and she doesn't like performing in front of large groups of people, but at least I get to enjoy her voice. She's also a fantastic cook; as you will soon find out. I got really lucky meeting her after the life I had been living."

At that moment Yvonne called us into the kitchen to eat. The spaghetti tasted delicious after not having eaten for hours. With fresh baked garlic bread, a tossed salad, and another beer, I was soon stuffed. This was much better than another peanut butter sandwich. Alan continued with the Scorpio attributes. He seemed intent on teaching me a lesson about my personality even if I didn't want to hear it. But why argue with a Hells Angel and possibly lose a place to sleep for the night?

"Sean, haven't you noticed how jealous you get around a woman you are dating? I bet if you ever really loved a woman you would be passionate about her and would do almost anything to get to see her as much as possible, like I did and still do with Yvonne. I also think you'd expect her to be just as serious about the relationship as you were. If she ended it, my guess is it would be like your heart was snatched from your chest and stomped on, right?"

"I, I haven't felt that kind of passion for anyone yet," I replied.

"Your eyes say otherwise, but I'll let that be," said Alan. "If it did happen I bet most people who were trying to be helpful said, 'just get over it' or, 'there's plenty of other women out there for you' or maybe, 'she wasn't that special'. Right? That's not how it works for Scorpios, believe me, I know."

Sometimes I wished I could just be rude and tell people to shut up, I'm tired of listening to your story, but instead I usually just nod my head and try to maintain focus. Plus, Alan and Yvonne were giving us a place to sleep and food to eat, being polite was about the only thing I had to offer in return.

129

After we all helped clean up after dinner Alan convinced Yvonne to sing for us. I was slightly embarrassed for her until she began an acapella version of "Amazing Grace". I thought how lucky Alan was to have such a caring and talented woman living with him despite his personal history with the Angels. Yvonne's voice was beautiful.

When she finished Alan said, "I can't tell you much about my time or exploits with the Angels, those things are for club members only, but let's go down into the garage and I'll show you the Harley."

I didn't understand much about the bike, but could appreciate how much Alan, or anyone else, would like riding one. I could see owning a bike myself in the future, except for the issue of car drivers who seemed to have a habit of hitting them.

Soon after that Alan and Yvonne went off to bed, while Paul and I unrolled our sleeping bags and slept on the living room carpet with Admiral laying between us. I'm not sure who snored louder, Paul, Admiral or me.

In the morning Paul and I did our sixty push-ups and sit-ups before a breakfast of Corn Chex, toast, and orange juice. It was great having clean clothes to wear again and roll into our packs. It was still a bit cool, so I stayed with jeans, a white t-shirt, flannel shirt, and sneakers, thinking they would be more comfortable on the city streets instead of hiking boots. Alan, Yvonne, and Admiral drove us near the Berkeley campus at the intersection of San Pablo and University Avenues, where they were sure another lift would be coming along quickly.

Several hitchhikers were already there, even though it was only seven a.m. I wasn't sad to leave Alan and Yvonne behind, but they were certainly interesting people and provided great food. The warm, dry, bug-free townhouse sure beat sleeping on the ground again. I didn't have to worry about any potato bugs crawling up my nose either. But it was time to travel north and think about heading to Canada.

Northbound

"Hey, who wants to go with me to Dallas, one person only?" asked a guy in a black Camaro with red flames painted on the hood and going down the sides. Paul looked at me and we both shook our heads no.

"Texas," I said to Paul. "That's too different from what I was thinking, someday I may get there, but not today, especially if we have to split up."

"I agree," said Paul. "Especially splitting up. Plus, before we left Brockport I promised my grandparents in Seattle I would stop to see them. You know, we have this new SEATTLE sign but people don't seem to be paying attention. Why would that guy think we would switch from Seattle to Texas?"

"I don't know. Either they don't care, they're stupid, or just not reading the sign," I said.

My radio was one of the best things I packed in Atlas and fifteen minutes later I was listening to KSAN from San Francisco playing Bob Seger's "Kathmandu", when a deep blue 1970 VW Beetle with a two-finger peace sign decal on the back window stopped. The goateed, late twenty-something looking driver said, "C'mon in, I'm going north to Redding."

"See, Paul, someone can read, the sign worked," I said.

Paul squeezed into the back seat with our packs and the Seattle sign, which wasn't easy in the limited space, and I rode upfront. An odor of grass engulfed the inside of the Bug and the driver immediately handed me a joint that had been sitting in his ashtray, which I gratefully accepted, who cared if it was seven-thirty? It made sense that the classic Grateful Dead song "Truckin" was playing on the radio. This had all the makings of a nice ride.

"Where are you two going?" asked the driver.

This question worried me a bit, so the guy really didn't read our sign, already let us get in the car after saying he was going to Redding, and now wants to know where we want to go? What the hell? Maybe the pot had already effected his thinking.

Paul let it go and gave our standard reply, "Seattle, then up to Canada and back to Upstate New York. We think with the Olympics beginning in Montreal soon there shouldn't be any trouble getting rides across Canada."

"Awesome, well, as I said, I can take you about three and a half-hours north to Redding, if you are lucky you might be able to see Lassen Volcano from the Interstate."

"That would be cool," I said as I passed the joint to Paul, who declined it. More for the driver and me. Paul was probably getting a buzz from the second hand smoke anyhow, even if he didn't want it.

"Hey, what's your name?" I asked as I handed him the joint.

"Martin. I'm a poli-sci teaching assistant at UCal Berkeley."

"Nice, so we should call you Professor Martin, right?" I said, taking another toke. "I'm Sean, an earth science major and Paul likes to dig rocks, he's a geology major. I took two political science classes last semester and loved them. My grades were better in those classes than any others. If I knew what to do with a political science degree I might get one."

"Jeepers Sean, you change your major all the time. Just stick to earth science or you'll be in school forever," said Paul.

"You could always be a professor, like me," said Martin, "or run for office, or maybe write speeches for candidates."

"I'm not that great at talking in front of classrooms, so I don't think I'd survive as a professor. I think I need a writing shed in my backyard like Roald Dahl, drink a bit of Bourbon, and learn to create special stories and characters. Maybe I can write articles about geology," I replied.

"Well, whatever, you have time to decide, I started out as a psychology major before switching to political science. So, sit back and enjoy the ride, in life and in my car. The Bug isn't big or fast, but it'll get us there."

Steppenwolf, "Hey Lawdy Mama," came on the radio, the windows were rolled down, and it was a beautiful, sunny, seventy degree morning as we drove along Interstate 5 through the middle of California.

I had to admit there were times hitchhiking was cool. If we got the right driver, a decent person with good intentions, who only wanted some company and to help another human being out, it was fun and exciting. With rides like this I could sit back, soak in the scenery, relax, and learn something new. I began thinking this summer experience should be worth three college credits in an independent English, psychology, or geography class.

We stopped at a USA Gasoline station near Willows, California. Paul bought a bunch of grapes, an orange, and a pint of strawberries at a farmer's stand next to the station. He was back on his healthy eating kick. I went for a homemade banana nut muffin and two apples. It was eleven a.m. when Martin left Interstate 5 for good. We walked across the street and onto the ramp heading back north, placing the SEATTLE sign next to Atlas. About thirty minutes later a light blue Volkswagen van with a white top drove onto the shoulder and waited for us to get in. Man there were a lot of VW's in California. An older man, at least forty, brown beard down to his chest, shoulder length hair, broad-shouldered, and wearing a plaid Simpson Logging Company cap, looked us over and said,

"I'm going to Seattle, hop in and let's get back on the road. We can be there in a few hours."

"Perfect," said Paul. "Exactly where we are hoping to get to today. My grandparents live there and we hope to spend a few days with them before heading back home in Upstate New York."

"Wow, New York, that's quite a distance to travel. My van might struggle a bit on the hills or mountains going through southern Oregon, but it'll get us there. By the way, my name is John."

"Well, that's Sean in the backseat and I'm Paul."

"Welcome aboard Sean, say hello to Brutus lying next to you on the seat."

Brutus, a Siberian Husky, seemed pretty calm about two strangers joining him in the VW. Even though I didn't own a dog, this trip was making me feel really comfortable having a calm animal sharing the seat with me. Brutus lifted his head to look at me and must have thought I was trustworthy, scooting over so his body was curled up next to my leg. Why did all these dogs like me? So strange. But Brutus made me feel like I was going to enjoy this ride.

133

"Look to your right and you can catch Lassen Volcano. Brutus and I are coming back from hiking and camping there for a few days. It was a nice little vacation for us."

"What are you vacationing from?" asked Paul. "I mean, what's your job?"

"I'm a logger, or lumberjack if you prefer. It's hard work but I enjoy being outside. Sitting at a desk all day isn't what I call fun. So, what do you guys do, besides hitchhike?"

"We're college students in New York. Paul is a football playing geology major and I'm a vodka drinking earth science major," I answered.

"Hah, vodka huh?"

"Well, I'm not too particular, beer, vodka, rum, I'm not really a fan of gin or tequila, but wouldn't turn it down if you're buying."

"Sorry, not this trip. What position do you play, Paul?"

"Center," said Paul.

"That's a tough position to play," said John. "I played a couple of years of defensive tackle at Eastern Washington before blowing out my knee. That's when I left college and started cutting down trees."

"Sorry about your knee," said Paul. "I've been able to avoid major injuries like that so far." The next couple of hours passed quickly as I actually fell asleep with Brutus's head resting on my lap. I don't think either of us moved an inch. My head was drooped over the seat back and drool coming out of my mouth when I heard John talk again.

"Looks like we've made it to the Manzanita, Oregon rest area," said John, as he signaled to leave the Interstate. "It's time for Brutus and me to take a leak. You boys can wait in the van or take care of business too."

"We'll go in," I said. "One of my mantras is to never pass up a bathroom when it's made available."

"Perfect mantra, I'm stealing that saying," said John.

John was still walking Brutus around the trees when I came out of the restroom area.

A vendor was outside selling Tillamook cheese and crackers. I wasn't a big cheese fan, but feeling starved, decided to buy a small block of cheddar. Might as well try what the locals eat. I also took advantage of the vending machines and bought a Payday bar, Coke, and a bag of Chex Mix. I wasn't sure what Brutus would eat, but hopefully it wouldn't be my food. Paul bought his own Tillamook cheese, along with a Dr. Pepper and a bag of Planter's Peanuts. John filled Brutus's water dish and after he laid back down on the seat next to me, gave him a bone to chew on, so my food was safe.

"Okay boys, buckle up. Now that we made it through Siskiyou Summit the ride should go a bit faster," said John. "Mind if I put on some music to pass the time?"

"Not at all," said Paul. For most of the next four hours, until arriving in Portland, we listened to Waylon Jennings, Johnny Cash, and Willie Nelson recordings. Not typically our first choice in music, at least in the bars Paul and I frequented, but it was tough to argue with listening to the Man in Black, especially when a rather large woodsman and his Husky were the hosts.

We needed gas in Portland, so John got off the Interstate north of the city stopping at a Texaco station, which coincidentally was next door to a Burgerville restaurant. Brutus had to wait in the van while we ordered dinner. A double beef cheeseburger, waffley fries, and another Dr. Pepper for Paul, two Northwest Cheeseburgers for John with a large double creamer coffee, two regular hamburgers with Burgerville spread for me (I was cheesed out from the rest area), fries, and the thickest vanilla milkshake I had ever had. I needed a spoon to get all of the ice cream out of the cup. John, fortunately, also bought two hamburgers for Brutus. I'm not sure who ate their burgers faster, Brutus or me. We continued to head north, soon crossing the Columbia River and into Washington. The end, at least for this segment of our trip, was in sight.

Michael McCullough

Seattle, Washington

John said goodbye as he exited I-5 onto state Highway 518 and headed home to the small town of Maple Valley.

"Hey, can I keep Brutus with me," I asked, half-jokingly, before John drove away.

"No, he goes where I go," said John. "Brutus and I are a team. I even take him to the logging sites with me. You two enjoy the rest of your adventure and stay safe."

***

Paul found a payphone outside a pizza shop and called his grandparents. It was 9:30 p.m., kind of late for old people to be driving around, but they weren't going to let us hitchhike to their house. Similar to the Millers, just not quite so far, the Davis's drove twenty-five minutes from Kirkland, a bit east of downtown Seattle, to pick us up and take us to their home. It was almost eleven p.m. before we arrived at their ranch home, only two miles from Lake Washington. I don't know what the elder Davis's had heard about me from Paul or his parents, but I wasn't getting an entirely welcoming feeling from them, not a hey, we really don't like you feeling, but not an entirely loving embrace either, it was like I had done something wrong. This trip was Paul's idea, not mine, I was just tagging along, and maybe they thought I was intruding on the adventure. I wasn't sure why they would be angry at me. I headed off to bed in a guest room after midnight, reading several pages of *One Day in the Life of Ivan Denisovich* before my eyelids wouldn't stay open. I could just slightly hear the voices of Paul and his grandparents as they shared family stories.

The next morning, Wednesday, July 14, I had to dig into the bottom of Atlas to find my overalls for the day trip we were taking to Mt. Rainier. Fortunately I still had a clean pair of socks and my boots didn't smell too bad. I wore my corduroy shirt again, figuring it would get cold on the mountain. Breakfast for me consisted of two bowls of Cheerios and two mugs of black coffee, it seemed these old people couldn't have some sugar coated, good cereal like Frosted Flakes or Frosted Mini-Wheats. I had to add a couple of spoonfuls of sugar to help the Cheerios go down smoothly. After eating we quickly left in the Davis's green 1972 Chrysler Town and Country station wagon for the two and a half hour trip. I had no idea how these old people were so awake and lively after being up past midnight. They were well over seventy years old and had more energy than me. If the scenery hadn't been so beautiful I would have fallen asleep during the drive. All during this trip I had the recurring theme that I may never be in whatever part of the country I was currently in again. I had to appreciate and try to enjoy each place.

We entered the park at the Nisqually entrance, passing meadows of wildflowers, deep forests, and always the mountain seeming to rise to the sky. We drove up to the Paradise Inn and the visitor center, already at 5,400 feet. I felt a strong desire to begin hiking, and the Davis's let Paul and I do the 2.5 mile Pinnacle Peak trail, where the view of Mt. Rainier was stunning. Thankfully I had purchased another cartridge of film from the gift shop before the hike. When Paul and I returned to the visitor center the Davis's bought us tuna sandwiches, potato chips, and Cokes, which we ate outside on a picnic table. It was another great day that I didn't want to end.

We arrived back at the Davis's home around seven p.m. Mrs. Davis had planned dinner ahead of time, only having to heat up a huge dish of baked ziti, garlic bread, and pull a pre-made tossed salad from the fridge. When she made all of this food remained a mystery to me, maybe it was something she had prepared before our arrival. After dinner we played euchre for a couple of hours before my energy level wilted. It was a shower and bedtime for me while the three of them stayed up talking until late into the night.

Thursday morning came early. For breakfast I mixed three heaping teaspoons of sugar with my bowl of Rice Krispies and slowly sipped a mug of steaming hot black coffee. Mr. Davis had gone shopping before Paul and I got up and made sure our backpacks were filled with peanut butter, apples, bread, fresh baked chocolate chip muffins, a Payday bar for me and Snickers for Paul, and a single-serving bag of Cheez-Its and potato chips for each of us. Mr. Davis must have thought Canada didn't have food we would like. We stuffed our clothes and food into the backpacks, got into the station wagon, and began driving to the Canadian border. My feelings about leaving were mixed. With the Davis's I felt like an outsider. They welcomed me into their home, but there was a wall between us that obviously was not going to come down, at least in a couple of days of getting to know each other. At this point I was also a bit anxious to begin the long trip home.

Michael McCullough

Border Patrol

As the four of us rode toward the United States and Canadian border in the station wagon I began to get increasingly nervous. I had only been in Niagara Falls, Canada with my parents a couple of times as a kid and was worried about the border crossing, especially being almost 3,000 miles from home. It was okay staying with Paul's grandparents in Seattle, especially the trip to Mt. Rainier, but I was ready to move on. There was something to be said for home cooked meals, sleeping in real beds instead of roadside ditches, having clean clothes, and riding in a car with people you could trust. It was like being back at the Miller's home in Colorado, except this time it was Paul who felt most comfortable. But it was also time to begin our trip back home and we just knew getting rides across Canada would be easy, what with the Olympics taking place in Montreal. It seemed natural everyone would give us a ride as they headed east.

Our immediate concern now, though, was how Paul's Methodist minister grandpa and his wife were going to get us through border patrol. Would they really lie about our purpose for going to Canada? What if the Canadians didn't want a couple of hitchhikers with hardly any money and from the United States in their country? I didn't know if my being confirmed as a Presbyterian made it easier to tell little white lies or that was my natural personality, but I couldn't fathom a Methodist minister stretching the truth.

Paul's grandpa brought the car slowly up to the crossing area and I could see the Canadian patrol guard looking curiously at us sitting in the back seat. The guard's chiseled facial features and official uniform with a pistol strapped to his waist made for an intimidating picture. I imagined him being the Canadian version of Officer Mahoney from Utah, except this guard had a Tom Selleck style mustache and a mullet hairstyle. The only identification Paul and I had were our New York driver's licenses. We hoped that was enough to get us through.

"What's your purpose for going to Canada today, sir?" the unsmiling, sunglass wearing guard asked Paul's grandpa. He leaned in through the car window and scanned to the back seat as he was talking. I just knew we were about to get busted, my paranoid mind was about to blurt out something stupid. We weren't even carrying anything illegal, but the entire situation was unnerving. I swear the guard was looking for a reason to pull us out of the car and begin a full body cavity search. But Mr. Davis just looked up and said;

"For the beauty of the earth,

For the glory of the skies,

For the love which from our birth,

Over and around us lies,

Christ, our God, to thee we raise

This our sacrifice of praise."[4]

 (Pierpoint)

"Wha, what was that sir?" asked the guard, "Are you a preacher or something?"

"Something like that," said Mr. Davis.

"Well, okay, how long are you staying in our country and are these boys staying with you?"

Boys! What was he talking about boys, we were men! I was getting tired of cops calling us boys, first outside the bar in Brockport, now at the border. Fortunately, before I could talk, Mr. Davis began again;

Then you will go on your way in safety,

and your foot will not stumble

When you lie down, you will not be afraid

when you lie down, your sleep will be sweet.[5] (Proverbs 3:23-24)

The guard took off his sunglasses, shook his head, wiped his brow, obviously frustrated and confused, looked the four of us over one more time and said, "Listen, sir, there is a long line of traffic behind you, just continue on and have a nice time in Canada with the family."

And that's how Paul's grandpa got us through customs, with the Lord's help. The Davis's reluctantly dropped us off near Surrey, outside of Vancouver, at the intersection of Highway 17 and the

Trans-Canada Highway. The long trek across Canada, 2,800 miles, was officially beginning.

[4] Pierpoint, Folliott. *For the Beauty of the Earth*. 1864.
[5]*The Bible*. Revised Standard Version of the Bible, Thomas Nelson, 1952

Michael McCullough

Cache Creek

Paul's promise of us getting rides quickly, and long ones at that, wasn't looking good. After being dropped off around nine a.m. by his grandparents we sat on the shoulder of the highway for an eternity. Even our new sign, EAST, TORONTO, wasn't drawing any attention. Maybe people in Canada really didn't care much about traveling more than 4,000 kilometers to watch the Olympics in Montreal. Maybe all these Canucks cared about was hockey, curling, ice skating, and downhill skiing? Curling, what a goofy sport. I couldn't imagine playing that unless I had a Molson beer in my hand and a belt with two more in the ready. One teammate would have to pull the cooler filled with beer around the ice. All of the summer sports seemed off the radar up here, which didn't bode well for rides. Why did the Canadian government even bid for the summer games?

I had my radio tuned to CKLG-FM which was playing Pure Prairie League's, "Two Lane Highway", when a vintage 1966, silver (except for several rust spots) Chevrolet C10 pickup with Alaska plates and a dented front bumper stopped. It was nearing twelve p.m. and I had already eaten the apple, muffin, chips, and Payday bar Mr. Davis had bought for me. The driver waved at us to come up to the cab. He was wearing a red Marlboro cap, a long-sleeved brown-checked flannel shirt with a pack of cigarettes in one of the pockets, jeans, and Carhartt boots. The hair sticking out from his cap, along with his beard, was turning gray. Sunglasses were laying on the dashboard along with a CAA map of roads in British Columbia. A hunting rifle was attached to the rear window. There was a loud bark and then an Alaskan Malamute stuck its head out the passenger window.

"Don't worry about Miska," said the man. "He's just curious about who I'm stopping for."

"Well, I'm Sean and this is Paul. We're trying to hitch across Canada and back to New York."

"If you don't mind sharing the cab with Miska, I can get you as far as Cache Creek, it's about a three hour drive, from there I head up Route 97, the Cariboo Highway, toward Alaska. Miska's a good dog, but not much for talking, I could use a bit of human conversation. By the way, my name's Caleb. You can put your packs in the bed of the truck with my gear."

Paul slid over to the middle of the bench seat and I took the door side. Miska had a carpeted mat on the floor to lay on by my feet when he wasn't half on my lap looking out the window. Once again I was the dog man. Caleb checked traffic and sped away from the shoulder; at least as much as a ten year old loaded down pickup truck could speed away.

"How far are you driving today?" I asked Caleb.

"Up to Prince George, five hours or so past Cache Creek. From there I still have around thirty hours of driving to get to my home near Fairbanks, so there'll be one or two more overnight stops."

"You have a lot of gear in the back, tires, gas cans, tools, cases of beer, and bags of dog food, does the ride get rough?"

"You have to be prepared, Sean, past Cache Creek there's a lot of nothing for a crazy amount of miles, I've learned from experience not to get caught short. Plus, while I'm down south in a big city like this, it's good to pick up supplies that are a lot cheaper than in Alaska. I went to Vancouver for twelve days, around July Fourth, to visit some family members, now it's time to head back north where I belong. Big city life isn't for me."

"What's your job in Fairbanks?" I asked.

"Oh, I'm a welder on the pipeline. The pay is good, though we work in all types of weather, which can get a bit rough. Sometimes I work seven days a week, twelve hours a day, even in the bitter winter months. But you have to take the money when you can, right? It's nice to come home to my cabin in Moose Creek, not far from Fairbanks, sit near the wood stove, read a book, smoke my pipe, and have Miska at my feet."

Paul must have been wiped out from the late nights and early mornings at his grandparents. He fell asleep with his head resting on the rear window while Caleb and I continued talking. I'd never met anyone from Alaska before, so this was a great opportunity to find out more about living in the state.

"In Alaska we rely on each other to survive. I don't know why you don't let Paul rest his head on your shoulder?"

"Ugh, I don't want him to touch me!"

"You wouldn't last long in Alaska, Sean. Sometimes you need other people to make it."

We passed through Hell's Gate, British Columbia. This was God's country. The Canadian Cascade Mountains, the Fraser River cutting through a gorge, stunning, beautiful scenery. This trip had its ups and downs, but seeing sections of the United States and Canada I might never see again was an unforgettable highlight. The names of small towns along the highway were unique, to say the least: Squeah, Spuzzum, Boston Bar, and Keefers. Near Spence's Bridge we continued driving along the Thompson River. We went through numerous small tunnels near the mountains. Paul was missing some special areas of Canada, but it didn't seem like I should wake him up. Miska had put his front paws on my lap and was looking out the window, which I opened up part-way for him. I think he wanted to stop and explore the land as much as I did. The day was warm and sunny. I was snapping pictures as we drove along the highway, not sure if they would come out blurry, but I had to try. When we neared Fishblue Lake I could see dozens of cars parked with people around my age drinking, swimming, and generally having a great time. It was another moment I was a bit sad to keep moving along instead of slowing down and joining in the fun. My desire to see the rest of Canada, a pull to want to go home, and having only thirty dollars left in my wallet, meant that extended stops would be non-existent.

"Have you always lived in Alaska?" I asked.

"No, I grew up near Beaverton, Oregon, west of Portland. I joined the Marine Corps in 1944 when I turned eighteen and was shipped off to fight on various islands in the Pacific Ocean. Guess I liked the Marines enough, the steady paycheck, and ended up re-upping, got trained to work as a welder and mechanic on anything that had an engine, and ended up in Korea for the war. Ten years was enough for me in the military, I had a little money saved up and heard about jobs and homesteading in Alaska, that's how I ended up with my sixty acres."

"My Dad joined the Marines when he was seventeen, in 1948, and served eight years, including going to Korea. He decided not to re-up a few months before I was born. I hope I'm not being too personal, but did you ever marry?"

147

"Oh, yeah, a beautiful woman, Isabella was her name. We met when I was stationed at Camp Pendleton, California, in-between wars. She was the nicest, kindest person I ever knew. She died of cancer about five years ago. Can't see ever marrying again."

"I'm so sorry, I didn't mean to pry."

"No problem, if I didn't want to answer, I wouldn't. It's good for me to talk about Isabella, I'm certainly never going to forget her."

Paul finally woke up when we neared the outskirts of Cache Creek. Caleb stopped at an A&W restaurant, which included a Chevron gas station. At the gas station mini-mart I bought three packages of orange Tang, two bananas, and a six-pack of Kellogg's Fun Pak cereal. Paul bought an entire bunch of bananas, three apples, and his own Fun Pak of cereal.

"Let's buy some real food at the A&W before we head back to the highway," Paul surprisingly suggested.

"I'm in, I'm starving and some hot food sounds great." I bought a chicken breast sandwich, onion rings, and a root beer. Paul bought a bacon cheeseburger, fries, and root beer, and Caleb got a bag of three hot dogs, two fries, and a large root beer.

"Don't worry, I'm sharing the hot dogs with Miska," said Caleb. "And I love their fries, they'll help keep me filled for the long trip ahead."

"Thanks for the ride, Caleb, I enjoyed learning a bit about Alaska," I said as I was feeding onion rings to Miska and petting his head. "Maybe I should keep riding with you and see what Alaska is like?"

"No, I don't think so, Sean, you keep heading back home and visit Alaska some other time. You two stay safe on the highway, I hope you get back to New York soon," said Caleb.

Paul and I walked slowly over to Highway One while we were finishing our food, it was after three p.m.

The rides weren't coming. It didn't make any sense. Did we really seem that threatening? Maybe we should have continued with Caleb and Miska to Alaska despite what he said. Maybe someone else would pick us up and take us north? We could have gotten a plane ride back to the continental U.S. once we were done visiting, or maybe never come back except to see relatives. We could have lived in Alaska, worked on the pipeline, finished college there, or maybe I could have earned my private pilot's license and flown a bush plane. Another one of those decisions that could be questioned forever. My life choices always seemed to hang on a spinning dime. Heads go to Alaska, tails, stay on the highway to home. I needed a seer or Magic 8 Ball to come along and tell me the future. Neither of those things were available in the Cache Creek Chevron station or A&W, so I spun a dime which landed on tails, meaning...go home you idiot.

Paul and I either walked back and forth on the ramp to Highway 1, or I sat on the pavement, whining, waiting for someone, anyone, to give us a ride while he threw stones at road signs. My butt was getting sore, so I began doing sets of ten push-ups and ten sit ups, over and over again. I shadow boxed round after round, I read more about Shukhov and the Soviet work camp. No one threw the bird at us, but they didn't stop either. Canadians were kind of nice, as their reputation was reported to be, but not nice enough to help us get closer to New York. This sucked.

***

It was past six p.m. when a black 1974 Ford Bronco pulled out of the Chevron station and stopped on the shoulder of the road next to us. A man and woman in their twenties offered us a ride to Kamloops and agreed to drop us off at Pineview Trails, a bit west of the city. Paul and I weren't sure what that meant except it got us further down the road. With the Bronco windows rolled down conversation was impossible without yelling so we didn't even bother sharing names. Pineview Trails turned out to be only an hour from Cache Creek, but still, a small step closer to home and much better than walking or continuing to stand on the roadside in Cache Creek.

The Kamloops area was a bit barren of trees and had rolling hills, hills that in Western New York would be mountains. The Thompson River flowed through the otherwise arid land, scattered with sagebrush and cactus, it was almost like a desert. We were nonchalantly dropped off after seven p.m. at the entrance to the Pineview Valley Park, half a mile from Highway 1. It was still hot, over eighty degrees, and as we walked to the park I began sweating like we were back in Brockport and it was football practice in full pads on a humid summer day. We didn't figure another ride would be coming this night, so Paul and I put our packs down and unrolled our sleeping bags on separate picnic tables. The Bronco couple had told us that black widow spiders and rattlesnakes inhabited this area, so I felt a bit safer being up off the ground, trying to believe spiders couldn't climb table legs.

"Might as well have our dinner of bananas and dry Fruit Loops, Sean," said Paul.

"It's fine. There doesn't seem to be any bugs biting me, yet, and it's finally cooling off a bit with the breeze picking up. It might be a decent night to sleep on a table. I'm still a bit full from the A&W and this isn't a bad spot to spend the night. I like it here more than some of the roadsides we slept next to in Kansas and Ohio," I replied.

"Yeah, one good reason to have you along is that you seem to be a bug magnet so they pretty much leave me alone," said Paul.

"Anything I can do to make you more comfortable, asshole."

I took my transistor radio out of Atlas and was able to pull up a local rock station. In the next hour we heard The Who's "Squeeze Box", KC & the Sunshine Band's "Get Down Tonight", BTO's "Takin' Care of Business", Anne Murray's "Snowbird", and Neil Young's "Cinnamon Girl." Paul kept reading his geology book and as darkness came on us I stared at the stars overhead trying to figure out the constellations. I wore a white t-shirt and kept my cutoff shorts on in case of a spider attack. My socks and sneakers were on the bench seat for a quick getaway, and my jackknife, with the blade already out, was next to the sneakers. I wasn't sure what kind of animal I could chase off or kill with a jackknife, but it felt better to be prepared. I kept my book, *Elements of Style* next to me to squash spiders with. Paul must have been worried too since he put his pick hammer on a bench. I used the rolled up tent as a pillow and fell asleep long before Paul, he was reading by flashlight when I last looked over at his table. His two hour nap in the pickup truck must have revived him for a late night.

A bright sunrise came over the mountains and immediately woke us up. A picnic table might have helped keep the creepy crawly bugs, snakes, and raccoons away, but really wasn't a soft surface for sleeping on, even with a pad under our bags. We did sixty push-ups and sixty sit- ups on top of the picnic tables, then ten wind sprints across the parking lot that seemed to be roughly fifty yards, half of a football field. It felt good to move my legs at full speed again. We were lucky that Canadians trusted its citizens and visitors enough to keep park bathrooms open 24/7. Paul and I carried our packs into the restroom, washed up, and shaved. Even at this early hour it was warm, so I changed my underwear, put the cutoffs back on, clean socks, sneakers, my Yellowstone t-shirt and Red Wing hat. Paul wore his geology shorts, sneakers, and geology club t-shirt. Paul dined on an apple, banana, dry Frosted Flakes, and water; while I mixed Tang into a canteen, ate a banana, and began munching on Apple Jacks as we walked to the highway.

Michael McCullough

Lake Louise

We got our packs and the EAST/TORONTO sign set up next to the guardrail on-ramp and as close to the highway as we could.

"I've been checking our map, Sean, it's only about a five hour drive to Lake Louise, around two-hundred seventy miles. From there it's two more hours to Calgary. Maybe we can make it to Calgary before nightfall," said Paul.

"That doesn't sound bad, but first we have to find someone nice to give us a ride. It's Friday, maybe someone will be vacationing in Lake Louise or Banff for the weekend and pick us up. Don't forget, we also lose an hour switching to Mountain Standard Time once we cross into Alberta."

I tried to sound positive, but really was worried about our chances of getting a lift and not ending up with another night sleeping on a picnic table.

We paced, sat, or stood on the shoulder of the on-ramp for hours. My thumb was wearing out. Paul and I took turns running back to the restroom, just in case a ride came along. We read our books and I wrote in my journal. When semis sped by I had to hold onto my hat so it didn't blow away.

"What if we begin walking down the highway?" Paul asked.

"Sure, and get to meet a Royal Mountie? I don't think so, especially after our run-in with the cop in Utah, I don't want to repeat that. I'm not sure how jails are in Canada and I don't want to find out."

Lunch for me consisted of a peanut butter sandwich with no jelly, Cheez-Its and more Tang. Paul ate another banana, an apple, and a peanut butter sandwich.

"That kind of lunch isn't going to help you gain weight for football, Paul."

"It's all I can do right now out in the middle of nowhere. It's okay, we'll be back home in a few days, I'll start pounding food, running consistently, and lifting weights again. I'll be in decent shape for the start of practice in mid-August. What about you?"

"I'm going to stick with lifting on my own, hitting the heavy bag, working part-time somewhere, maybe I'll take a class in strength training, earn a couple of credits for exercising," I replied. "I just don't think I can get heavy enough to play on the line in college ball and I'm not fast or quick enough for other positions. It's okay, I've come to peace with my decision."

"That's too bad, I think you're being lazy and giving up too soon, you never know what'll happen over the rest of the summer and when practice starts."

"Yeah, that's true. Right now I can't see it, but we'll see."

At that precise moment a sage green 1973 Volvo station wagon pulling a pop-up tent camper stopped fifty yards from us on the highway. A thin, tall, athletic looking woman, with a ponytail that went half-way down her back, and appearing to be in her thirties, got out of the passenger side door.

"Need a ride?" she asked.

"Yes, we do," Paul exclaimed.

"Going to Toronto I see," she said as we got closer to the Volvo. "We can get you to Lake Louise, then you'll have to stay the night at their campground or continue to find other rides, okay?"

"Perfect," said Paul.

An equally thin, athletic looking man with long black sideburns and a short beard, cautiously got out of the driver's side door so a passing car wouldn't hit him and met us at the tailgate.

"How ya doin? I'm Daniel and this is my wife, Cheryl. We left Vancouver early this morning to take a ten day trip to do some climbing in the Lake Louise area."

As we put our packs on top of their equipment, Daniel closed the tailgate and Paul stuck out his hand, introduced himself and I followed suit, then we all got into the car. I immediately noticed a smell of Ben-Gay wafting through the car and a tube was sitting in the front ashtray.

"We've driven through here numerous times, you guys are going to love this area," said Daniel. "It's one of the most beautiful areas in Canada, maybe the United States, too, as far as I'm concerned. Have you guys been to the Tetons? The mountains around here are like the Tetons on steroids."

"We hitched through Grand Teton National Park on our way to California after staying in Yellowstone, I wish we could have stayed in that area longer," said Paul.

"How long have you two been hitchhiking, where have you been out on the road?" Cheryl asked.

I decided to try and sum up the long story of our travels:

"We started in Western New York, near Rochester, stayed in Windsor, Colorado, a bit north of Denver for a couple of nights. We were able to tour around Rocky Mountain National Park with a couple of friends. From there we ended up in Yellowstone for a couple of nights, then got rides down through Utah, over to Big Sur on the California coast, up to Paul's grandparents in Seattle, finally over to Vancouver, which brought us to you two. We're heading back home now, trying to follow the white and green maple leaf route markers."

"Wow, that's quite a trip. We've actually hiked in Rocky Mountain National Park, the Tetons, and Yellowstone," said Cheryl.

"That's so cool," said Paul. "What jobs do you have that let you travel so much?"

We had driven past more interesting named villages, Shuswap, Squilax, Sorrento, Balmora, and finally we took a break at Salmon Creek on the shores of Shuswap Lake, stopping at another A&W restaurant.

"These places are everywhere," I said.

"Yeah, they're pretty popular in Canada," said Cheryl.

"If you look to the south, that's Mount Ida, they call the hills back to the west the Fly Hills, and across the lake is Bastion Mountain," said Daniel, before answering Paul's question. "We both work at Grouse Mountain ski resort, in North Vancouver. We get a lot of time off during the summer months, which is why we can travel and hike so much. It's a great gig. Cheryl is a ski instructor and I manage the bar when I'm not out skiing."

Paul and I both ordered Papa Burgers, with a side of onion rings, and root beer. Daniel ordered two bacon double cheeseburgers, two orders of fries, and a root beer. How did he stay so skinny? Cheryl had a chicken tender sandwich and root beer, avoiding the greasy rings and fries.

Daniel filled the Volvo up with gas at the nearby Chevron station, saying, "You can't be too careful out here, especially when we get into the real mountains, there isn't another reliable place for food or gas for quite a while."

As we continued heading toward Revelstoke we passed deeply forested rolling hills and crossed the Monashee Mountain range, driving through, or near, more diverse village names: Sicamous, Malakwa, and Craigellachie. For many miles we followed the Eagle River as the highway kept twisting and turning, going by Three Valley Lake, Three Valley Gap, and Victor Lake Provincial Park. In the distance Daniel pointed out Mt. Griffin, Mt. English, and Mt. MacPherson.

"Cheryl and I have climbed MacPherson," said Daniel.

"Did you know on Mt. Copeland, near Revelstoke, they set a Canadian record for one season of snowfall?" said Cheryl. "It was only four years ago, the 1971-72 season, twenty-four meters, or about eighty feet, that's 963 inches of snow! The poor village had 779 centimeters, or as you Yanks would say, 307 inches. It covered the roofs of a lot of houses. Twenty-five feet! Imagine that."

"I thought Upstate New York was snowy, with our 100" or so average, three to nine times that is not the kind of winter weather I want to be in," said Paul.

"Me either," said Cheryl. "And I'm a professional skier."

We made it through Revelstoke, on the banks of the Columbia River, without incident and began the trek towards Lake Louise. The highway went through Rogers Pass, known to be prime black and grizzly bear country, it would have been cool to see one, but only from the car, not up close and personal. To the east of us were the Selkirk Mountains and Glacier National Park. We headed toward Golden, British Columbia, going through Kicking Horse Canyon and several tunnels, which Daniel told us were snow sheds to protect the roadway from avalanches. The Kicking Horse River paralleled much of the road. We passed a sign for Yoho National Park, Chancellor Mountain, 10,715', Mt. Vaux 10,860', and the Waputik mountains were within the park.

"Man, I cannot get over these mountains, they are so crazy high, still snow covered near the peaks, I've just never seen anything like this, except in books," I said.

"Yeah, they are spectacular, our plans are to camp in Lake Louise and Banff for the next ten days and hike to the summit of a couple of the peaks," said Cheryl. "We usually see deer, elk or moose on our hikes, which is always exciting, if not also a bit nerve wracking. Too many hikers act like the wild animals are tame pets and not an actual danger. It's the bears though; we really have to be careful if we see one of them!"

"Bears, yeah, we, or me anyhow, kept talking loudly on the trail when Paul and I were hiking in Yellowstone. I was pretty worried about running across one."

"Understand, he's worried about all wild animals, including every mosquito in the world," said Paul.

"Well, what do you and Daniel do about bears?" I asked.

"Oh, I'm a faster runner, so I don't have to worry as much as Daniel, I'll just take off and let the bear get him," joked Cheryl. "No, really, talking, clapping, or singing is a decent strategy to warn them you are coming and not accidentally sneak up on a Mama bear, that's the worst. We both carry bear spray and if we were to encounter one on the trail, would walk backwards, but not look the bear in its eyes. We might talk quietly too, so the bear knows we aren't a threat, but are humans. Then you just pray to whatever deity you believe in."

"Good advice, thanks. Hopefully we won't have any encounters on future hikes," I said.

Before Lake Louise we crossed into Mountain Standard Time, losing another hour. Daniel and Cheryl dropped us off on Lake Louise drive so we could go into the small grocery store for some food.

"Thanks for the ride and all the information on the mountains and bears," said Paul. "Have a great time camping and hiking!"

"Goodbye and good luck with the rest of your trip across Canada. We hope your rides come quick and take you far," said Cheryl.

The small, local, grocery store had everything we needed for the night. We bought a twelve pack of ice cold Molson beer, two family sized bags of chips, a hot, medium-sized pepperoni pizza, and sat at a picnic table outside the store to devour our food and two beers apiece. It was a one kilometer walk to the campground on Fairview Drive, where we were assigned a site for only five dollars. Paul and I pitched the tent while drinking another Molson, rolled out our mats and sleeping bags, put our packs inside, grabbed two more Molson's and hiked the four kilometers to see the Lake. The campground was surrounded by fencing designed to keep grizzlies out, which was both reassuring and worrisome. Lake Louise was a crystal clear glacier fed lake that Paul and I just stared at, admiring its beauty while finishing another beer. We could see Mt. Niblack at 9789', Mt. Temple at 11,627', Mt. Fairview at 9,008' and several other high peaks. It seemed like they touched the heavens.

We walked back to the campsite, finished off our chips and beer, and went to sleep almost immediately. It was strange how stressful and tiring it could get waiting for some stranger to pick us up.

The next morning, Saturday, we put on our respective cutoffs, hiking boots, and I wore my Earth Science club shirt. Paul wore his plaid short sleeve shirt. We packed the rest of our gear, hiked back to the village, bought a breakfast sandwich and orange juice for each of us, refilled our canteens, and walked across the Bow River to the on-ramp.

Calgary

It was only a two hour drive from Lake Louise to Calgary. Paul and I began standing at the on-ramp to Highway 1 at eight a.m., Saturday, July 17th. Our late start was due to each of us having a bit of a hangover from the twelve-pack we shared the night before, moving slowly when packing our gear, and still getting used to the time change. We propped up our EAST/TORONTO sign next to Atlas. It was a Saturday morning in July; wouldn't everyone be traveling past Lake Louise to get to Banff, or better yet, Calgary and beyond? Anyhow, those were our thoughts. It took two more hours to get a lift, which was ridiculous considering the number of cars that entered the highway via the on-ramp and drove by us. Finally, an aqua blue 1973 Ford Econoline van with a Calgary Cowboys bumper sticker stopped next to us on the ramp. A deeply tanned man, appearing to be in his 60's, got out and walked toward us. A gray ponytail stuck out the back of his red and white Calgary Cowboys cap. He was wearing gray hiking shorts, L.L. Bean moccasins, calf high white socks, and a brown flannel shirt.

"Heading anyplace special, guys?"

"Yes, sir, trying to hitch back to New York," said Paul.

"Hmm, that's quite a trip, I can only get you to Calgary, my hometown. My name is Christopher, and you two are?"

"Paul and Sean," I answered.

"Pleased to meet you, one can ride up front, one on the bench seat," said Christopher. "Just watch out for the mean dog in the back, she can be real trouble."

"Ah, well in that case Paul would be glad to sit on the bench seat, I'll watch the scenery up front."

Paul took our packs and placed them in the back of the van. The mean dog turned out to be a cute, little, black Scottish Terrier named Duff. Other than raising his head to look at Paul, Duff stayed in his dog bed and waited for the van to start going down the highway before falling back to sleep. The mountains were still gorgeous during the drive and all I wanted to do was to watch the forests, river, and mountains as we tooled down the road, thinking what a shame it was that we couldn't spend more time here. Once we got past Banff it was only a ninety minute drive on the four lane highway until downtown Calgary. Fences lined the side of the road to help keep wildlife from wandering onto it and causing an accident.

"Today is opening day at the Olympics in Montreal," said Christopher. "Are you guys interested in them at all? Personally I can't wait for the real action to begin. I'll watch any of the sports they show on television, but my favorites are gymnastics, equestrian, and track & field, especially the decathlon."

"One of the reasons we chose to hitch across Canada to get home was the Olympics. We thought rides would be easy to come by, with lots of people heading to Montreal," I said. "So far it really hasn't worked out quite the way we envisioned. But, yeah, we are both into sports, love the Olympics. The first time I remember watching them on television was 1968, the Mexico City games. I remember Jim Ryun winning the silver medal in the 1500 meters and the U.S. announcers acting like he had a terrible race, that he should have won the gold. Even at eleven years old I thought they were idiots. On that day Ryun was the second fastest runner in the world at that distance, not too bad in my book."

"That's nice of you to say, Sean, I recently retired from being an assistant coach with the Medicine Hat Tigers in the Western Canada Hockey League. Coach Shupe and I always wanted to have the young men give their best effort during each practice and game. Winning was great, loved winning, we won the championship in the 73-74 season. But we needed to develop the players for possible NHL careers too."

"Was there an age requirement for the team?" I asked.

"Generally sixteen to twenty years old, though a fifteen year old could play if he was really talented, but only for five games unless their midget level team's season had ended. So, do either of you play hockey?"

"No, I play center on the college football team," said Paul.

"Oh, well you must be quite an athlete then," said Christopher.

"I work pretty hard at it," said Paul. "Lifting weights all year, never missing a practice, attending spring training, I think all that helps."

"What about you, Sean?"

"In high school I was on the football and tennis team, and I always stayed after school for weightlifting, gymnastics, and basketball, anything the gym teacher offered and let me keep moving. I was cut from the college tennis team, but play lots of basketball and other intramural sports, including broomball on the hockey rink."

"Broomball?"

"Yeah, it was coed, we wore sneakers and used brooms to pass a small ball to each other and try to score. It was a lot of fun and a lot of falling on the ice."

"Interesting, we just skate up here, usually kids start around the same time as when they begin walking."

"Yeah, kind of weird, living in Upstate New York with some terrible, cold, snowy winters, and I never learned how to skate. But I've gone to quite a few Rochester Amerks hockey games and our college team, the Brockport State Golden Eagles, are pretty exciting to watch."

"Amerks?" We've actually had a few players end up in the American Hockey League, including playing for or against Rochester, that's great."

We were entering the Calgary city limits and Christopher began maneuvering the van around from one lane to another.

"I'm dropping you off in the city center at a spot where a lot of hitchhikers seem to stand and wait for rides. Hopefully someone comes along quickly."

"Sounds great," said Paul.

When Christopher stopped the van we could see a couple of hitchhikers thinking he was going to pick them up. He waved them off as Paul and I got our backpacks, patted Duff on his head, and thanked Christopher for the lift. Calgary at last... only 2,200 miles to go!

Michael McCullough

Katherine

There were five other people looking for rides within two blocks of us in downtown Calgary. We had no plan of where to sleep in the city if we didn't get a lift soon. It was a hot and humid afternoon when out of nowhere a brown 1974 Jeep Cherokee pulled toward us. As the driver leaned over to the unrolled passenger door window, long brown hair cascaded down past her shoulders over a green blouse and her blue eyes looked up at me. She appeared to be in her mid-thirties.

"Where you headin' to, eh?" she asked.

"As far east as you can take us," I said.

"I'm going down Highway 1 to Brooks, just under two-hundred klicks, will that do it?" Her voice sounded soft and cool, I had visions of a gently flowing mountain stream. I was anxious to climb in the Jeep for a ride.

"Absolutely, we're ready to go," I replied.

We placed our backpacks in the rear storage area in between sacks of cat food and litter. Paul rode shotgun, I got the rear seat all to myself next to Loblaw grocery bags filled with fresh fruit and vegetables. The Jeep, or maybe the driver, smelled woodsy, like I had stepped into a deep pine forest. After being surrounded by the stuffy, humid air of Calgary, with bus diesel fumes wafting in the air, this was a comforting relief and I was looking forward to another nice, relaxing ride. At least we didn't have to worry about sleeping on some city bench or back alley anymore.

"Well, give me your names, stories, where you're from, where you're going, I want it all," she asked. "It's a three hour drive and we have lots of time, I'm Katherine, by the way, and work as a nurse in the local clinic in Brooks."

Before Paul could answer and dominate the conversation I spoke up. "That's Paul, I'm Sean," I said in an attempt at a calm, confident sounding voice. Katherine, I thought, such a nice name. Any Katherines I had known were intelligent, self-assured, warm, positive people; though in all honesty I had only talked to two women named Katherine in my life.

"We've been doing kind of a circle route, beginning in Western New York, to the California coast, up to Vancouver, and now heading back home," I said. "We've been gone about three weeks so far."

"Wow, that's quite a trip, tell me more," Katherine asked, as we made our way out of the city center and onto the main highway.

"Wait, before you begin, there's two bags of Cheezies in one of those grocery totes, Paul and I will share one, you eat the other one back there, okay?" she asked. My stomach had been growling in hunger for a couple of hours, so I had no problem grabbing some food, even if I wasn't sure what Cheezies were. Turns out they were just the Canadian version of Cheetos, which was fine with me. For someone whose back seat was filled with fruits and vegetables it seemed a bit odd to be offered junk food for a snack, but I wasn't going to argue.

A thousand thoughts and images went through my mind as I decided which experience she would most appreciate. Seeing the cat food and litter in the rear of the Jeep made me hope Katherine would trust us a bit more if I told a story about a chicken farming ex-boxer as we rode together in the expanses of Canada.

"We were in the middle of what seemed like nowhere Utah, struggling to get a ride, hoping someone would pick us up before the cop came back," I began.

"Cop? Why would the police be after you?" Katherine asked, in a concerned voice.

"Oh, no worries," I said quickly, and explained about the citation for standing on the Interstate and threat of being tossed in jail for vagrancy in Spanish Fork, Utah, which Katherine agreed seemed rather extreme.

"Finally an older man pulled over and told us to climb in, which we gratefully did," I continued. "He seemed powerfully built, even when wearing a jacket, with thick calloused fingers and a square jaw. We put our packs on the back seat when the man roughly said, "don't let the kittens out!" Paul shrugged his shoulders as we looked at each other. Neither of us saw or heard any kittens in the car or running around outside. I began to wonder about this guy's sanity. Should we get in or not? Paul took the back seat, looked up, and said, "It looks like your kittens are all here sir, there's a bunch of them in the box on the floor."

"There should be seven of them, can you count them?" the man said more warmly.

"Yep, yes, they're all here, seven kittens in the box," said Paul.

"Good, that's good, now we can drive."

Paul stayed in the back seat of the sedan and I took the front seat. The man told us his name was Raul and he was a chicken farmer outside Salina.

"I'm Sean, this is Paul," I said. "We're headed to California."

"I can get you as far as Scipio, that's my exit, that's it," he said. "It's about seventy miles down the highway."

"We're good with that, appreciate the ride." He began to open up and relax more now that we had kept his kittens secure in the car and Paul was gently petting one in his lap.

"The kittens are a surprise for my wife and six kids," Raul said. "I wasn't always a chicken farmer; I used to be a professional boxer. I was a welterweight, took a few punches, you may have noticed my nose being a little out of whack?"

"It was your huge hands and forearms I actually noticed more, but now that you mention it your nose is a bit flat and crooked," I said.

He just laughed and shared stories about fighting Joey Giardello and Emile Griffiths, champion middleweight boxers in the 1960's. He had saved enough money from boxing to buy a small ranch and begin a new career, safely away from anymore uppercuts to the jaw or hooks to his ribs. The seventy miles went by quickly. A man of his word, Raul and his kittens dropped us off at the exit to Salina, near a Big Boy restaurant and Sinclair gas station.

"Not a bad story, Sean," said Katherine. "It sounds like Raul had quite an interesting life, from boxing to chicken farming with a love of his family, bringing home all of those kittens, that's sweet."

"Yeah, you just never know who'll give you a ride. Everyone always has a story to tell and it's hard to know what it is by looking at them," I said, wondering what Katherine's story would ultimately end up being.

***

Instead of dropping us off on the shoulder of Highway 1 outside of Brooks, Katherine invited us to spend the night at her rustic log cabin built by her and family members. Maybe my ex-boxer turned chicken farmer story made her more comfortable about trusting us. Paul and I simultaneously said yes without even checking with each other first. I wasn't about to lose this opportunity to spend a night with a woman after Paul ruined it with Mary Ann back in Indiana. We turned off the four lane highway and the last road sign I saw was Route 873. Suddenly we took a left turn onto a tree-lined, dusty, rutted, dirt lane that Katherine nimbly drove the four-wheel drive Jeep along.

We came up on a one story wooden cabin with a nice covered porch and a pond off to the side. The cabin was surrounded by woods and no other homes seemed to be nearby. Katherine parked near the cabin and the three of us carried all of the groceries, cat supplies, and backpacks inside. The cabin had electricity, a wood stove for heat, and running water in the kitchen, but no indoor bathroom. Besides the small kitchen, there was a dining room table, and, near the wood stove, a well-used but comfortable looking couch, a coffee table with piles of magazines, and two rocking chairs.

Before we could get settled in, Katherine said, "Who's volunteering to help me with the water hose?"

I had no idea what that meant, which didn't matter since Paul immediately said I would do it, the bastard. The skills I learned at home repair were having my father call an expert, usually a Masonic buddy who overcharged him, to come fix whatever was wrong at our house, Dad certainly wasn't going to do it. From the porch Katherine grabbed a pair of big rubber boots that went to her knees, gave me another pair, and we headed toward the pond I had seen when we first arrived. It was three times the size of an in-ground swimming pool, filled with water and surrounded by boot sucking, calf high mud.

"Pick up the hose, would you?" Katherine yelled, acting like I had some idea of what the hell we were doing or what part of the long black hose I was supposed to be grabbing. I was standing in the mud about twenty feet from her and just reached down and grabbed the hose from the mud.

"Okay, now what?" I asked.

"Hold onto it and pull it into a deeper section of the pond while I hook this end up to the pump. It must have come loose and it's our only water source for the cabin," she said.

It began to rain. The brown sludge turned to quicksand. My feet slipped repeatedly, but at least I didn't go down.

"Is this our shower water, drinking water, or what?" I asked.

"Yes."

"Yes, we drink this?" I asked.

"Yes, don't worry Sean, it's clean, I had it tested," Katherine said.

"It's a mud hole, what do you mean, clean?" My sarcastic, frustrated self was coming out.

"Hey, do you want to go back onto the highway and stick your thumb out right now," Katherine shot back.

"Umm, well, I can see you're right, it must be clean since we're five miles from the nearest town and half a mile from any neighbors. Yeah, I'm ready for a drink."

"Besides, I don't have an indoor toilet, you may have noticed the outhouse over there," Katherine stated, pointing toward a clearing with a small outbuilding about twenty feet from the front porch. "The cabin drains can only be used for sink and shower water, someday I'll have a septic system hooked up, but there's no rush and it's really expensive."

We slogged through the mud and back to the cabin, the water line intact. Katherine and I found Paul sitting on the couch reading a copy of Maclean's magazine he found on the coffee table, a cat laying on his lap.

"I see you've met Chloe," said Katherine. "She loves staying warm and taking naps on laps."

Paul kept petting the cat and asked, "Can I help cook anything for dinner?"

"Nope, we're going to Tim's Bowling & Billiards in downtown Brooks to meet a few of my friends, drink a few stubby's, and you can order anything your heart desires to eat, paying for it yourself, of course," stated Katherine. "Get cleaned up and ready to go, we leave in ten minutes sharp."

"What's a stubby?" I asked.

"A Labatt's of course," answered Katherine. "A small, fat bottle."

"Ah, well I'd like a couple of those, for sure," I replied.

I changed into the best outfit I had, my flannel shirt, overalls, and sneakers, brushed my hair and was ready to go. Paul came out of the spare bedroom, which he had already declared as his for the night, wearing jeans and a Barge Inn/Stumble Out t-shirt.

"I'm ready to party," he said, smiling. Katherine came out of her bedroom wearing bell bottom jeans, a white blouse covered by a denim jacket and black ankle high leather boots. Seeing her walk through the cabin made my heart rate go up a few beats, but I remained outwardly calm. We got into the Jeep and headed toward downtown Brooks.

A few minutes later we pulled into the parking lot at Tim's and walked directly to the bar. Friday night at eight p.m. and the place was hopping. Paul bought the first round, three stubbies and three shots of Harwood whiskey. The night was shaping up nicely. We grabbed a table in the pool hall area and met Kathryn's friends; Kevin, Tom, Robyn, and Carla.

I was too hungry to be polite and stick around for small talk, so I headed back to the bar and ordered my dinner, a double burger, large fries, and another stubby. The others could get their own food. I was starving and grabbed two bowls of bar nuts to eat while waiting for my burger and carried them back to our table. Paul and I stood near the pool table enjoying our beers, munching on nuts, and watching Tom and Kevin play eight ball. In the background I could hear Robyn and Carla pestering Kathryn with questions about us. The Doobie Brothers, "Rockin' Down the Highway", was playing on the jukebox.

An hour or so later, after we had all eaten and survived another round of shots courtesy of Kathryn, an Olympic preview show was on one of the barroom televisions. Kevin began talking smack about the USA team.

"You guys only win medals because the government pays the athletes to train and compete," he started. "The Canucks get nothing except a uniform when they make the team. Food, a training center, coaches, all free for the United States athletes. Our people are lucky to get running shoes and equipment," he continued.

The nonsense talk was making me crazy. "You mean like our marathoner from 1972, Frank Shorter?" I asked. "He trained with friends in Florida, had to get food stamps so he could eat, and shared a two bedroom apartment with three other guys and still won the gold medal. What kind of advantage is that over your Jerome Drayton? Or how about Bruce Jenner, our best decathlon athlete who had to sell insurance to pay his living costs while training for the Olympics this summer?"

Kevin didn't want to hear it. "You Yanks have all the advantages in Olympic sports, I don't care what you say. I know what the truth is." I wasn't in the mood to continue arguing, there didn't seem to be a point to it other than Kevin drunkenly spouting off and ruining the night.

"Hey, let's play some eight ball instead," I challenged. "You can even break first." I knew he couldn't beat me, even after three shots of whisky and four beers. Paul knew what I was up to and played along,

"C'mon Sean, you've had too much to drink and won't be able to play better than a third grader," he said.

Carla laughed and said, "Kevin, you'd better beat that Yank or you'll never hear the end of it."

Kevin gruffly grabbed his cue stick, chalked it up and said, "Let's go hoser, and I'm first, you can stand there and watch me run the table!"

I chuckled to myself and said, "hey, keener (I only knew that slang word after hearing someone say it at the bar and hoped I was using it in the right context) let's put some money on it, winner gets five dollars." I slapped my five on the pool table.

Kevin said, "No problem," and put his five down too.

Kevin had a decent break, but didn't sink any balls. I made a couple of shots, and then purposely missed. Kevin made three in a row before missing, then I missed again. He ended up winning the game fairly easily and grabbed the money.

I just winked at Paul and said, "Let's go again, I get to break, we each put in a ten." Kevin saw an easy mark and agreed, but made it even better, saying, "Let's make it twenty." The jukebox was appropriately playing "Clowns to the left of me, jokers to the right" by Stealers Wheel, one of my favorites.

I hesitated and told Paul I needed to borrow ten dollars, "no way hoser," he said. So I dug deep in my coveralls pocket and came up with another ten dollars of my own. Now there were forty dollars on the pool table up for grabs. I racked the balls myself to make sure it was done correctly, placed the cue ball to the far right, aimed at the ball on the fourth line, added a bit of backspin and hit it firmly. Not surprising to me a ball went into the side pocket. I chalked the cue stick and proceeded to calmly run the table before Kevin could get a shot off. I grabbed the forty dollars and went to the bar for another shot of Hanover's for Paul, Katherine, and myself, still pocketing a profit of fifteen dollars after leaving the bartender a tip. It was a good night. Kevin didn't bring up the Olympics again, or much else, preferring to sit at the bar and nurse a beer. Paul kept the conversation going at our table while I watched a Canadian Football League game between the Calgary Stampeders and the Edmonton Eskimos and stayed pretty silent. Around midnight Katherine announced it was time to go home, so we got into her Jeep and took off.

Even I could tell my body was encrusted with road funk, some remaining dirt from my battle with the pond hose, and smoke from the bar. I took the first turn in Katherine's outdoor shower, not caring about conserving the hot water from her solar water heater. It was like heaven. I could pick out the constellations Hercules to the north and Scorpius to the south on this warm Canadian summer night, the rain clouds from earlier in the day had drifted away, and I didn't even need a flashlight since there was a full moon. What a great time to enjoy an outdoor shower. After drying off I put on a t-shirt and pajama pants, went back into the cabin, said goodnight to

Paul and Katherine, and crawled into my sleeping bag on the couch. It was so comfortable, a quiet night out in the woods, a gentle breeze flowing through the window, and Chloe sleeping above me on the top of the couch. I could stay in this cabin for days. I felt like I was a kid again, staying at my grandmother's cabin deep in the woods overlooking Canandaigua Lake in New York. I half expected Paul to move into Katherine's bedroom, but he didn't, I think the whiskey and stubbies had caught up to him, as his snoring grew a little loud.

In the middle of the night I had to pee, and trying to hold it until morning so I wouldn't bother the two of them wasn't an option. With no indoor bathroom I had to slip on my sandals and run to the outhouse hoping there wasn't a bear or some other wild animal out there that would eat my ass. As quietly as a mouse, or so I thought, I snuck out the door and took care of business.

As soon as I got back into the cabin I heard Katherine, "Chloe didn't get out did she?"

Shoot, I tried to be so quiet. "No," I said.

"Are you sure?" she asked. I wasn't, the damn cat had moved from the couch, but a few seconds later, which seemed like minutes, I found Chloe at her water dish and grabbed her in my arms. "No, I have her; do you want me to bring her to you?" I asked.

"Yes please," she said. Katherine's bedroom door opened and she was standing there in light brown pajamas decorated with pine trees and had scuffies on her feet. I placed Chloe in her arms. Part of me, of course, wanted to ask if I could sleep in there too, but at the same time it seemed like I would be trying to take advantage of her, which I didn't want to do. Katherine had been so nice to us, I didn't want to ruin that trust, so I said nothing.

"Goodnight," whispered Katherine.

"Goodnight."

I went back into the living room and got comfortable again on the couch, falling asleep quickly in the quiet of the woods. When I woke in the morning Katherine was in the kitchen cooking. Whatever food she was making smelled delicious. Paul and I started to do our sixty push-ups and sit-ups, which got a bit hard when Chloe decided to lay under me when I was doing the push-ups. I had to be careful not to squash her. After forty push-ups I couldn't take it any longer and went over to sit at the table and drink the fresh brewed coffee. We ate some omelet configuration loaded with all varieties of vegetables that in normal times I never would have tried. Paired with warm, homemade bread I was in heaven, it was absolutely delicious. Katherine could cook. Maybe I could stay in the cabin with her and become the handyman of the place, even if I wasn't all that handy. I was still trying to find my place in the world, maybe Brooks, Alberta Canada, was it?

"Okay guys, it's time to get back on the highway," said Katherine, stopping any thoughts I had about staying there. "Let's get the cabin cleaned up, you two can pack and we'll be ready to hit the road. I'll take you up the highway to Medicine Hat, about 109 klicks, then you'll be on your own."

The mountains were long gone, far to the west of us. Now we were in a flat as pancake farmland. I thought Kansas and eastern Colorado were flat, but nothing compared to this. It was a difficult parting, at least for me. Katherine almost acted angry, like she wanted us to go but wanted us to stay at the same time and didn't know how to say that. Paul and I graciously thanked her for everything, hoisted our backpacks and held out our thumbs, as Katherine drove away up the road to a U-turn area and waved at us as she headed back to Brooks.

Breaking Up is Hard to Do

Meant to live alone?
Alcohol, pot, my old friends
I could use you now.

So we sat. And we sat some more. Medicine Hat, what kind of name was that? Canada had the strangest town names ever. I understood that some of them were adaptations of native names, or maybe the true native name, that made perfect sense. But Medicine Hat to an ignorant college kid from Upstate New York seemed more than slightly ridiculous. We really didn't learn a lot about Canadian history in high school. I knew more about the geology of the land, thanks to my earth science classes, than anything else. All I could think of was Professor Hinkle in "Frosty the Snowman" and his magic hat. Magic Hat, Medicine Hat. A weird connection, but that's the way my brain worked.

Katherine, boy I missed her the more I sat on the shoulder of the road. A clean, comfortable, quiet cabin outside a small town. A nice woman who cared about our well-being, fed us, gave us a place to sleep and delicious food, what more did I need? A steady girlfriend might be nice, but who knew if that would ever happen. I did know that sitting on another pebbly road shoulder breathing exhaust fumes, wondering why all these assholes wouldn't pick us up, was not it.

It was the summer Olympics for Christ sakes. Didn't these Canucks care at all? If the Olympics were in Chicago I would have gone there from New York. Why weren't these people going to Montreal? Why weren't they picking up two hot, good looking athletic guys, with a sign, backpacks, and our thumbs out? Obviously we weren't bums. We were even wearing our cutoff jean shorts and boots, showing our long, tanned, athletic legs, ha-ha, c'mon already! This made no sense. Maybe it was my hat, like anyone up here knew what a Rochester Red Wing was. Maybe they didn't like my shirt. But who doesn't like Poe? Maybe it was Paul's shirt, his stupid SUNY Brockport football shirt, with his guns popping out of the sleeves? Up here it was all ice skating and hockey and that goofy "sport" curling. We should have been carrying hockey sticks, slung skates over our shoulders, and wearing Gordy Howe shirts.

Rain clouds began to move in. We had to put our ponchos on. Paul and I had been out here for hours with no rides. People weren't even throwing us the bird or pretending to hit us with their car, it was just one driver after another ignoring us. So far from home, out in the Canadian prairie, kind of knowing where we were, but not really. It was all strange territory. In a way we were trapped, little cash, no car of our own, we were at a loss of what to do.

"There's a campground right there, Paul," I said. "It's starting to rain, it's late, we can at least pitch the tent, stay dry, and try again in the morning to get a ride."

"Yeah, that's probably not a bad idea. I can't believe no one will pick us up. It's crazy," agreed Paul. We reluctantly slung our packs on our backs and hiked the short distance to the Gas City Campground. We were able to get a tent site without an issue and quickly set up camp. Paul scrounged up some wood and started a fire while I went to the camp store, bought a pack of hot dogs, rolls, and a six pack of Molson. The store clerk gave me a few mustard and relish packs for free. We were in business.

Maybe it wasn't the most nutritious dinner, three hot dogs and three beers apiece, but it filled our stomachs. We listened to tunes on my radio, CJCY-FM while eating dinner. The music wasn't bad, a cross-section of rock songs, like Marshall Tucker's "Can't You See". Paul began talking about rides, or lack thereof, and suggested it might be best if we split up in the morning and see what happened at the same time Jim Croce was singing "Movin' me down the highway, rollin' me down the highway".

"I am getting tired of sitting on the shoulder all day," I agreed. "Maybe that's the best thing to do right now. Let's see what the morning brings, rides and sunshine I hope."

There were bathrooms and showers at the campground, but I was too lazy, and, after all, had showered the night before at Katherine's, how dirty could I be? We fell asleep listening to light rain falling on the tent. The morning sun was a blessing as we packed our gear, but the ground was still a bit wet from the previous day's rain so we skipped our push-ups and sit-ups. That was fine with me, I was depressed and concerned over splitting up to care about exercising. It was a bit cool and my cutoffs were damp, so I put on jeans and my earth science shirt with hiking boots and the Red Wing hat. Paul stuck to his cutoffs, boots, and geology club shirt. Breakfast consisted of the last of our dry cereal and Tang. We refilled our canteens with water from the campground. After washing up we flipped a coin and Paul won, meaning he could try and get a ride first while I hung out close to the campground.

"See you later, Sean, I bet we will end up in one of the towns up ahead and be able to hitch rides together soon." It wasn't more than fifteen minutes later I saw Paul get into a 1973 brown Chevrolet Nova. He waved back at me, and, with a smile on his face, threw the bird, the fucker. Now it was my turn to hit the highway.

Michael McCullough

Regina

Three hours after Paul rode away, while I was listening to my radio and Blind Faith singing "Can't Find My Way Home," a canary yellow 1974 AMC Hornet slowed down, put on its turn signal, and pulled over next to me. The driver, a curly blonde haired male, who looked to be in his thirties, rolled down the window and said, "I'm heading home to Regina if you want a ride."

"That sounds great!" I said, and placed Atlas in the backseat and I sat up front. I rolled up the window halfway as we merged onto the highway.

"I just filled up the gas tank, so we shouldn't have to stop unless it's for the bathroom."

"I'm looking forward to the ride, thanks for picking me up. We've had a tough time getting rides recently, so this is nice."

"We?"

"Oh, I've been hitchhiking with a friend across the United States and Canada, but we split up this morning thinking it would be easier to get a lift," I said. "By the way, my name is Sean."

"Eh, I'm Brian. That sounds like an incredible amount of miles to travel. Where did you begin?"

"I live in Upstate New York, near Rochester. We started there, made our way to California, then up to Seattle, and continued to Vancouver, then began back home on the Trans-Canada highway. We've been gone over three weeks."

"New York, hmm. Lots of skyscrapers and buildings all close together?"

"What? No. New York City is probably a six hour drive from me. I live more in farm country, a small suburban town. Nothing at all like New York City. It's more like around here, all these farms and flat land. Well, not quite like this, far more prairie land and oil wells around here. But I definitely don't live in a big city."

"I guess you don't hear about that part of New York, it's easy for people living up here to only think of the City or maybe Niagara Falls," said Brian.

"This might not be my business, but what took you to Calgary if you live in Regina?" I asked.

"Oh, I work for the Saskatchewan Wheat Pool; it's a cooperative of farmers. We try to ensure fair prices are paid, among other things. I do quite a bit of traveling to different cities and towns."

We continued driving past towns with names like Piapot and Gull Lake.

"Piapot, that's a strange name for a town, what does it mean?" I asked.

"It's pretty much a ghost town, I don't think it has much more than a post office, maybe a couple of dozen people live there. It's named after a Cree Indian chief."

Throughout this trip I had been in awe by the mountains, but in a strange way the endless prairie land was just as striking. It wasn't an area I would want to live in, but traveling through here, at least for a first timer, was enthralling, it was so expansive, as far as the eye could see, just flat land going and going. We stopped in Swift Current at a rest area. I was glad for the break, even if it was brief. At the vending machine I bought a small, hot black coffee, a Coffee Crisp bar, and a bag of Cheezies, which made me think of Katherine. I seldom drank coffee before hitchhiking. I always loved the smell of it in the mornings at home, but now it seemed a necessity to actually drink and I was beginning to develop a taste for it. The caffeine seemed a necessity on so many parts of this trip. We continued driving, passing the towns of Morse, Mortlach, and finally Moose Jaw. Brian told me Morse was named after the inventor of the telegraph, Samuel Morse, even though he was an American. Mortlach was a Scottish parish name and not one of the post-human races from *The Time Machine*, the Morlocks, by H.G. Wells, as I thought, and Moose Jaw had nothing to do with moose, but was an adaptation of a Cree word meaning warm breezes.

We entered the city of Regina around 9:30 p.m. Brian dropped me off at the Southland Mall parking lot, not far from the Trans-Canada highway. It was virtually empty of cars on this dark, cloudy, forbidding Monday night.

"Route 6 is right there," said Brian, pointing to the east. "If you head south you'll be in the U.S., if driving, in less than three hours. If you go north, well, you can see the Regina downtown buildings, maybe you can find a place to stay. Sorry I can't be of more help. I wish you luck on your travels. It's about twenty-five hours driving to Toronto if you stay on Highway 1."

"Thanks for the ride, Brian, I appreciate the help. I'm sure I'll be okay."

With that I was left standing alone in a parking lot, fifteen dollars in my pocket, no map of the Canadian highway system, since I had stupidly forgotten to bring one, half a jar of peanut butter for food and not sure what to do. Three hours back to the U.S., even if it was North Dakota, was appealing. But Paul had said we needed to take the Trans-Canada highway back home. I was feeling lonely, and lost, really lost, for the first time on this trip. Survival was in my hands. Paul could be a hundred miles ahead of me for all I knew.

I found a pay phone outside one of the mall stores and called home. Well, not home. I called my brother, collect, thinking maybe he could give me advice or at least make me feel not quite so lonely.

"Hey, thanks for taking the call, I'll make this quick and pay you back for the charges when I get back home."

"Where are you?" James asked.

"I'm near Regina, Saskatchewan, still about 1,800 miles from home. It looks like a pretty big city. It's closing in on ten p.m. here. Sorry to call so late."

"You know that's no problem. Jeez, that's still a long way to go. Is Paul there with you?"

"No, we decided to split up earlier today; it was taking so long to get rides in Canada. We thought going separate might work out better. I don't know where he is, except he was picked up before me. The guy who dropped me off here said I can walk downtown, but it's probably three or more miles away. There's also a road that goes toward North Dakota, but that's a three hour drive. I'm not sure whether to try that and at least get back to the United States, or keep going on Highway 1 through Canada."

"Why don't you find a place to stay there tonight," James suggested. "How much money do you have?"

"Fifteen dollars."

"That's it? Not much. You still have Dad's charge card?"

"Yeah, how did you know he gave me that? I haven't used it at all. I know I'll have to pay him back for anything I charge, plus interest," I said.

"I think it would be worth it to have a hotel room to stay in for the night, if you can find one, then decide in the morning what to do," said James.

"Okay, sure, that sounds good I guess. I don't think I'd get a ride at this time of night anyhow, at least not from anyone I'd really like to be traveling with. There's no place to sleep near this mall and I'm kind of tired of ditches on the side of the road. Thanks. Hopefully I'll see you in a few days. Tell Mom and Dad I'm okay."

"Will do. Good luck. It'll work out," said James.

With that I hung up the phone, put Atlas on my back, and began walking north to downtown Regina.

Regina - Part II

I made my way over to the sidewalk next to Route 6 heading north and began looking for a place to stay. Looking south on Route 6 it seemed to get desolate quickly and I didn't see any cars heading in that direction. I didn't relish spending the night out there. Still, it was eerily quiet on the outskirts of the capital of Saskatchewan. Miraculously I came to a small motel after walking for only fifteen minutes. It was called the Midnight Sun and looked clean and safe enough from the road. I went inside the lobby and the woman behind the counter raised her right eyebrow, frowned, and stared at me like I had just crawled out from under a bridge, did I really look like a troll?

"May I help you?" she asked.

"I was hoping to get a room for the night," I replied. In my mind this would work out well. This place was only a few minutes away from Highway 1. I could easily stay the night and get back to the road in the morning, or get on Route 6 and head back to the States.

"We don't have anything available," she said.

"No rooms at all? I said as my heart sank in my chest. "I have a charge card, I can pay for it. There's a vacancy sign out front."

"I said we don't have anything for you. Maybe you need to keep walking downtown, try one of the bigger places."

"Thanks for nothing," I mumbled as I turned around and walked out the door. I knew she was lying. It was a Monday night, how many people were really staying here on a Monday? The parking lot wasn't even half full. Did I really look or smell that bad? Put out the no vacancy sign if you are really full. Asshat.

The street going north looked endless. Every once in a while a light post would help guide me as I was walking. My energy; emotionally, mentally, and physically, was waning. The Cheezies and coffee had worn off long ago. Using my jackknife to eat from the peanut butter jar didn't seem like the greatest option at this point. There was no place around here where I was going to be able to sleep on the side of the road or a park that might have a picnic table to lie on. This trip had been great but was taking a dark turn. Eighteen hundred miles from home, what was I going to do?

I made my way across a bridge, which according to a sign was above Wascana Lake and Wascana Creek. A public park may have been around the small lake but in the late night darkness I couldn't tell for sure and there was no obvious path. It was still a long walk to downtown, especially when I had no idea where I was or where I was going. The streets were quiet and no one was out walking, who would be at this late hour on a Monday night? After more than an hour of being scared of my own shadow I made it to a high-rise Marriott hotel in the middle of downtown Regina. It looked really fancy, too fancy for someone like me, road weary, backpack over my shoulders, smelly, I figured it was 50/50 they would call the police on me for being a vagrant. After taking a deep breath I walked up to the reservation counter where two women were working, it was around eleven p.m.

They raised their heads to look at me, one was on the phone and the other one, a thirty-something year old blonde with a Dorothy Hamill haircut named Margaret (according to her nametag) said without hesitation, "Do you need a room for the night?"

I was in heaven. I could smell her perfume from across the counter; it had a hint of melon, a nice smell which helped make me feel welcome and hungry. What a difference in attitude from the previous motel clerk.

"Yes, absolutely, thank you! Actually, come to think of it, two nights might be better since it's so late. Here's my charge card."

"Great. We can take care of this quickly. Do you have identification to go along with the charge card?"

"Yeah, I have my driver's license."

"Perfect. Sean, nice name. From New York, wow, you are a long way from home!" Margaret stated.

"I've been doing a lot of traveling, New York to California, to Vancouver, and now I'm heading back."

"Wow, that's amazing, good for you. Okay, sign here, two nights; the total will be sixty-two dollars Canadian with tax included, or about sixty-five dollars U.S. We have a restaurant on the other side of the lobby. It opens again at six a.m. Here's your key, you'll be on the eighth floor, Room 812. The elevator is right there," she said, pointing behind me. "Enjoy your stay, Sean."

"Thank you, I think I will."

With that I took the elevator to the eighth floor and walked to my room. It was beautiful, at least to someone used to sleeping on the side of the road, on top of picnic tables, or in my two man tent. This was much better than finding a spot near Lake Wascana and sleeping on the ground or a picnic table. I had a queen size bed, a huge television, and, opening the curtains, a view of the city. I turned on the Olympics, stripped off my clothes, and climbed into a hot shower. The road grunge ran brown off my body and down the drain. I hadn't realized how dirty I actually was. After drying off I washed some of my clothes in the tub with my remaining Wisk detergent and hung them up to dry. I climbed into the cozy bed, pulled the covers up to my neck and watched boxing and basketball highlights for an hour before falling into a deep sleep.

Tuesday morning I woke up around nine a.m. to a knocking at my door, almost nine straight hours of sleeping. I looked through the peephole to see the maid standing in the hallway.

"Wait a minute please," I said and quickly put on a shirt and shorts and let her in. My hair was uncombed, tangled, and flying in all directions; plus I needed a shave.

The maid looked a bit uncertain as to what to do, finally asking, "Do you need me to vacuum, empty the garbage, or maybe you'd like a fresh towel?"

"I'll just take a towel, thank you," I said. "I came in late last night; there really isn't any garbage or reason to vacuum."

"No problem sir, here you are, enjoy your stay," she said. Sir? Wow, I'd never been called a sir before. This was a fancy hotel.

I closed and locked the door, opened the curtains and looked at the view of the city before turning on the television to watch the Olympics. I went down the hallway to fill up the ice bucket so I could have a nice cold glass of water in my room. Having nothing else to do I took off my clothes and laid in bed under the covers, wondering what to do next. I was already booked for another night, but then what? Back to the highway and hitchhiking? I still had no map to really know where I was. Regina was a big city, the capital, so I could check on flying back maybe? But that would be too expensive. What else was there? A bus or the train? Hunger pains motivated me to get up, do my sixty push-ups and sit-ups, get washed, brush my teeth, and get dressed in my Yellowstone park shirt, jeans, socks, and sneakers. Finally I left to find food.

At the hotel restaurant I asked about using my credit card and was pleasantly surprised when the hostess said my breakfast cost would be added to the room bill. Another reason to like this place.

She led me to a booth, handed me a menu, and said, "Your waitress is Janine, she'll be over in a minute to take your order."

It was easy to pick out what I was going to eat, especially since putting the cost on the charge card felt like eating for free, even though Dad would make me pay in full plus interest when the bill came in the mail. While waiting I looked around at the other customers and realized I was the youngest by probably twenty years. It appeared I should have been carrying a briefcase to fit in with the business people in here. Oh well. At least this was one time it didn't feel like everyone was staring at me, they all seemed to be absorbed in the daily newspaper or quiet conversations.

"Hello," said Janine, a twenty-something looking woman with shoulder length straight blonde hair and deep blue-eyes, "are you ready to order?" She was wearing the standard Marriott pink and white blouse with a knee length white skirt and apron and smelled like maple syrup, but maybe that was my hunger imagining the odor.

"Yeah, I'll have the Oilman's special, with a small orange juice and coffee."

"Decaf or regular?"

"Regular, I need some caffeine, lots of caffeine."

"I'll put your order in and bring the coffee right over."

"Great!"

True to her word, Janine brought the coffee over in a few seconds. Newspapers were free at the hostess station, so I walked over and joined the other patrons in staring at the articles in the Regina Leader Post, though I went right for the sports section. I was in no mood to read any bad news articles and didn't really care about

Regina news anyhow. A few minutes later Janine brought my juice and a full stack of pancakes and sausage.

I took a chance and told Janine that I had been hitchhiking across the United States and Canada, then asked her, "If you didn't have a car and couldn't afford airfare, how would you travel from here to Niagara Falls, or at least Toronto? If you were me, would you keep hitchhiking, take the train, or maybe a bus?"

She put her left hand on her hip and right index finger on her chin and thought for a minute before saying, "the bus is cheaper than the train, but it's going to be a long trip, there's an express that leaves every day from downtown, the station is only a few blocks from here. You know more about hitchhiking than me. It's always a risk wondering when you'll get a ride and with what kind of person, isn't it? I guess I'd go for the bus, just bring a book or two, some food, and water." She wrote directions to the bus station on a napkin.

"Thank you." With that I dug into my food, suddenly realizing I hadn't had a real meal since hot dogs at the campground with Paul on Sunday night and now it was Tuesday morning. The pancakes were gone before Janine could refill my coffee mug. I left a two dollar tip, which seemed more than fair for a three dollar meal, and began walking to the bus station to see what a ticket cost.

The Greyhound station was less than a ten minute walk from the hotel. The diesel fuel was a familiar, sickening smell that engulfed the entire terminal. I walked up to the ticket counter and asked the chubby-faced male clerk about the express bus to Niagara Falls.

"We have a bus leaving tomorrow morning at seven a.m., July 21, going to Niagara Falls. It's the Express, traveling along the Trans-Canada highway, costs thirty dollars U.S, and takes twenty-nine hours. Are you interested in purchasing a ticket?" he asked.

"Twenty-nine hours, that seems incredibly long. Is there anything faster?"

"Look, it's 2,700 kilometers, or almost 1,700 miles to you. Not a particularly short distance and the price is cheap. Do you want a ticket or not, there are people waiting behind you in line."

"Yeah, okay, I'll buy a ticket. Here's my charge card and ID. What time should I be here in the morning if the bus leaves at seven?"

"Be here by 6:40 so the driver can load your luggage and take your ticket. We leave on time around here."

"I'll be here." With that I took my ticket and felt semi-satisfied with the decision to continue home by bus instead of hiking to the highway and trying to hitch a ride.

I walked back to the hotel, again noting what streets to take and checking landmarks so I wouldn't get lost in the morning and miss my bus. At the hotel I went back to the reservation desk to ask how to get cash using the charge card.

"It's easy, Mr. Matheson, we can give you money, it'll be added to the card and in your next bill."

"Fantastic," I said. "I'd like forty dollars please."

With the influx of new cash I walked outside and found a small convenience store. I bought a loaf of rye bread to go with my peanut butter and a pack of maple leaf cookies for the bus trip. Back at the hotel I wandered around to check out what else was here I could use for the next few hours. There was a pool, a hot tub, a couple of meeting rooms, and an exercise room. I loved this place. I went up to my room, changed into my gym shorts, black muscle shirt, sneakers, and headed back to an empty exercise room. There were a lot of dumbbells, no barbells, so I concentrated on bicep curls, triceps, single arm rows, shoulder presses, and crunches. I tried a few times to do chin ups, but, as usual, sucked at them, barely getting six completed in three sets and those were shaky. Despite that it still felt good to have a real workout after weeks on the road. I missed being in a weight room. The weight rooms in high school and college were my sanctuaries.

It was early afternoon before I got back to my room, showered, and dressed into normal clothes. I turned on the Olympics again and was able to watch gymnastics, wrestling, weightlifting, and boxing. Nadia Comaneci was continuing her string of perfect 10's in gymnastics. Around six p.m. I headed back to the hotel restaurant for dinner. The hostess led me to a booth, and, surprise, Janine was my waitress again. She still smelled like maple syrup. I was beginning to think she drank it instead of coffee, or rubbed it on for perfume behind her ears.

"Back for more, I guess breakfast was okay then?" she said.

"Breakfast was great, and thanks for the advice on choosing the bus, I bought a ticket and will be leaving here by 6:20 a.m. so I can make the seven a.m. departure time."

"Oh, good for you, I hope it works out. Here's your dinner menu. What do you want to drink besides the water?"

"7 Up would be great, thank you."

I looked over the entire menu before choosing the meatloaf special, with mashed potatoes, green beans, gravy, and a roll. It was another good meal, I was afraid it might be my last real meal for at least two days so I used the roll to sop up every bit of gravy. I made sure to stay around long enough to thank Janine for the meal and bus suggestion, gave her another two dollar tip on a three dollar meal and went back to my room.

The clothes I had washed the night before had finally dried. Always one to prepare ahead of time, I laid out my jeans, clean socks, boots, underwear, and my Grateful Dead, "keep on truckin' t-shirt. I called down to the desk for a 5:40 a.m. wake up call. I didn't entirely trust the room alarm clock, but I did set it for 5:40 a.m. too. It was only eight p.m., so after showering again I turned on the television to watch more of the Olympic Games, and sat in the chair next to the window so I could see the night sky over Regina. There were more diving, boxing and wrestling matches on. I wrote in my journal to help pass time. There were advantages to making all of my own decisions, but also a deep, lonely feeling. I turned off the television and fell into a restless sleep after eleven p.m.

The alarm went off a few seconds before the front desk called. I quickly washed up, shaved, brushed my teeth, got dressed, filled my canteens with water, and packed Atlas. Once in the lobby I had to wait a couple of minutes before paying the bill. I was getting nervous about making it to the bus on time, kept glancing at my watch and rocking side to side.

The desk clerk said, "There's free coffee and your choice of a doughnut or muffin on the table behind you, why don't you take one of each before leaving?"

"That sounds like a good start to the day." I put a peanut covered doughnut and chocolate chip muffin in a paper bag, filled a coffee cup, and took a peek in the restaurant to see if Janine was working so I could say goodbye, but didn't see her, so I hurried to the bus terminal. Of course, being anal about being late, I was in the terminal at 6:25 a.m., plenty of time to get checked in, give Atlas to the driver, and pick out my seat.

"Looks like you've been doing some hiking," said the driver, as he was placing my pack in the storage compartment under the bus.

By now I was a bit tired of telling the story of all the places I had traveled, but being polite and not needing to piss him off, I said, "I've been hitchhiking across the U.S., came up to Canada, but I guess got a little tired after 5,000 miles of relying on the goodness of others for rides and decided to be lazy and take the bus back to New York, the state, not the city."

"Hmm, well I can understand that. Do you need anything from the pack before I put it in here? This is going to be a long trip."

"Oh, sure, yeah, thanks for asking." I took out my radio and headphones, sunglasses, hat, journal, a pen, and Kerouac book. I was out of film so there was no reason to keep my camera, besides, why would I want photos of my bus ride? I watched as the driver carefully packed Atlas in with some other luggage, then climbed aboard and took a seat in the third row next to the window. I stretched out my legs on the other seat; I wanted to be left alone.

Before the driver sat down he said, "Good morning everyone, I'm Rodney and will be your driver for your trip from Regina to Winnipeg. Enjoy the ride.

I was happy to discover the Greyhound Express bus had a bathroom in the back. The bus was only half full when we left the station at seven a.m., just like the clerk said it would.

Express?

Lord too far too slow
into the night help me go
sucking diesel fumes

Being a bit naive about transportation methods, or maybe the English language, I was under the impression express meant fast, swift, rapid, high-speed and the like. Apparently I mistook the adjective meaning of express: "traveling with few or no stops in between" [6] (Merriam-Webster) with the Greyhound bus meaning of: "We are going to stop at every goddamn little town and big city along the way, you mister former hitchhiker be damned! Sit there and enjoy the ride, read your stupid book, good luck picking up a radio station out here in nowheresville you stupid little man." That saying must have been in Greyhound's mission statement, but I had missed it in the excitement of being off the shoulder of the road wondering who might take pity and pick me up.

Really, the bus came to a stop in every fucking town on the route; Indian Head, Grenfell, Whitewood, Moosomin. I guess those fine citizens had every right to catch a bus from Moosomin or wherever, but couldn't it be a normal bus, not the "Express"? I wanted to get to Niagara Falls, not have a tour of bus stops in small towns across Canada, no wonder it was a twenty-nine hour trip. This was already torture and Moosomin was only two and a half hours from Regina, actually more riding the bus due to the previous stops.

Maybe the bus driver had a weak prostate and had to use the bathroom in every town. Two of the stops no one got on or off, why would they? Grenfell? Really? No offense to the citizens of Grenfell, I'm sure among the eight hundred or so people living there quite a few of them were fine people, but I wanted to keep moving fast.

[6] "Express." Def. 3a. *Merriam-Webster's Collegiate Dictionary*. 7th ed., 1972.

A few miles before the town of Elkhorn we entered the province of Manitoba and the central time zone, the same as Chicago. That fact helped me finally feel like we were making progress, even if it was inch by inch. I moved my watch forward another hour.

When the bus reached the town of Brandon, Rodney said, "it's mandatory break time for me, you can get off the bus and walk around, but be sure to be back on in twenty minutes. We leave whether you're on or not. There are bathrooms and vending machines in the terminal."

I decided to stretch my legs and use a normal bathroom instead of the bus one. I had eaten the doughnut and muffin the hotel had given me and emptied my canteen. The vending machines provided pretty typical fare, but I did buy a two pack of Hostess cupcakes as a snack for later. I figured my main meal for the day would be a couple of peanut butter and bread sandwiches. I refilled the canteen at a drinking fountain and went outside to stretch for a few minutes. Feeling cooped up from sitting on the bus, I got down on the little bit of lawn that was available and knocked out three sets of twenty-five push-ups. Most of the other passengers kept smoking and stared at me like I had lost my mind.

We all got back on the bus when the driver came out of the break room. A few seconds after I had gotten comfortable in my seat a bum stumbled onto the bus, looked around, and chose the seat next to me! Crap. There were plenty of empty seats further back on the bus, why me?

"Hellllooo," he wheezed. "Gonna be a good day, right, young fella? Figure I'm riding to Winnipeg, then maybe spend the night there before moving on, what about you?" It was hard to tell his age, forties, fifties, I wasn't sure. He had a three day growth of beard and a really dark tan, or was it dirt encrusted on his taut, worn skin, who knew? His pants were a russet color; he wore a red corduroy shirt with a moth-eaten, wool, brown suit jacket and a light brown painter's beret hat. His teeth were yellowed, at least the ones he had, and he smelled like tobacco smoke and whiskey. All I knew was I didn't want to be sitting next to this.... gentleman for any length of time. It could have been I was out of empathy for others, or wanted to be left alone (which was true) or maybe I was looking into my future self and found it repulsive and scary.

Two elderly women, who had been sitting behind me since we left Regina, also looked disgusted with our new passenger. I could see them talking to each other, holding their noses and pointing to my new "friend." At that instant the gentleman reached into his jacket pocket, winked at me, and pulled out a pint of Black Velvet whiskey. He offered me a sip, which I declined, and began to drink. It was around 11:30 a.m. Fortunately for me the driver was getting on the bus, I waved to him and pointed at my seatmate. His reaction was swift.

"What do you think you're doing? Get off my bus now! There's no drinking and no drunks on MY bus! Get out!"

My seatmate staggered to his feet and looked back like he wanted to punch me, but only threw me the bird. I was getting used to people throwing me the bird on this trip. I felt a bit guilty, but only a little, as he gingerly went down the bus steps and out onto a bench near the station where he sat slouched over. If he had sat anywhere else on the bus I wouldn't have cared. I was in no mood at that time to be friendly and smell someone who smelled worse than me.

The elderly ladies bent forward, saying, "Thank you young man for making him leave, we didn't trust him near us."

"He smelled so bad I didn't want him sitting by me," I replied, stretching out my legs. With that we began our trek toward Winnipeg. Of course we couldn't drive the two and a half hours straight to Winnipeg; the bus made a stop at Portage la Prairie first. At least at this stop a couple of people disembarked and three new passengers came on board. We arrived at the Winnipeg station at 2:10 p.m.

"This is my last stop," said Rodney. "I'll be changing to a bus heading back to Regina, where I live. Your new driver will take you to Thunder Bay, with stops in-between, of course. There's a bathroom inside the station, but be sure to be back on the bus by 2:25."

Ten people, including the elderly women who had been sitting behind me, were done with their trips. Only six new passengers came on, giving us twenty-nine total riders out of fifty-eight seats. I continued my Harriet the Spy routine, observing the station surroundings and especially my fellow passengers. I was curious about where they lived, what life was truly like in Canada, and why they were riding the bus. Niagara Falls, Canada was only seventy minutes from Brockport, and that was my total experience with their "culture", a tourist town. A woman sitting in the row opposite me looked to be about thirty. She had long, shiny, black hair that went down her back, almost touching her butt, deep brown eyes, and a child that appeared to be around two or three years old sitting next to her. She was quite pretty. I was guessing she was a teacher or maybe a farmer's wife, it was hard to tell. In the seats directly behind the driver sat a young couple, probably in their twenties, who were holding hands with her head laying on his shoulder, looking like they were deep in love, at least until one cheated on the other or didn't really know what love meant. He was probably a struggling poet and she was a veterinarian assistant. Behind me were two females in their fifties who wouldn't stop talking about politics, the weather, their new grandchildren, and a myriad of other topics. I was happy to have my radio and earphones to block them out. I was guessing they were best friends going to a high school reunion. The rest of the passengers were just as diverse: college age students, business people, single men and women, covering all ages, races and ethnicities. It made for a more interesting ride, using my imagination to make up stories about all of these people. I began to take notes on them in my journal thinking I could use the material in creative writing classes back at Brockport State.

"Hey everyone, I'm Stanley and I'll be your new driver. We should be in Thunder Bay at eleven thirty, which includes the time zone change near Raith, about an hour from the end. Let's get going, okay?"

Stanley hooked his Greyhound cap and jacket on a pole next to his seat and slid in, making adjustments to accommodate his stumpy legs. With that I put my earphones in and found a decent radio station, 98.3 FM, sat back, and tried not to think about the long road ahead. The station only came in for about an hour, but I did hear music from Janis Joplin, "Me and Bobby McGee" singing about being busted flat in Baton Rouge, which sounded like me, except I was closing in on Thunder Bay on a bus, but still busted flat. It seemed like a sad night song for me because next came Eric Clapton and "Bell Bottom Blues" yeah; I want to beg to take her back, sure, like I hadn't done that enough times already. A few songs later was Electric Light Orchestra's, "Evil Woman" which was how I felt about a former girlfriend. Soon after that my signal died, which was probably for the best. I could only take so much sadness, even if they were good tunes.

The scenery was interesting, at least as far as I could see in the fading light, appearing to be lakes at every turn in the road. One of the largest was Lake of the Woods near Keewatin, but they continued through Vermilion Bay, Dryden and Gullwing Lake, and Ignace. As Stanley promised we hit the Thunder Bay station on the edge of Lake Superior at 11:30 p.m. I had been on the bus for over fourteen hours with the time changes. It was getting to be old sitting on a bus for so long. I needed to move my legs, stretch, run a little, and play some basketball or tennis, anything to feel like blood was flowing in my veins again.

Express? - Part II

We had twenty minutes before the bus left again so I went into the station to use the bathroom. On the way out I noticed a map of the area and our route to Niagara Falls. Lake Superior and then Lake Huron went on forever and Highway 1 stayed close to both of them. The highway was never going to end. The Canadian province of Ontario was massive. I was going to be on this bus till the earth was destroyed by a giant meteor and killed everyone like the extinction of the dinosaurs. Only cockroaches and Greyhound Express buses would survive the apocalypse. It was over 900 miles till my ride was done, about sixteen more hours with stops. At least we were in the Eastern Time zone, but it still meant not arriving until Thursday at four p.m. Ten passengers got off the bus permanently and two new ones came on. When Stanley opened the storage area before leaving for the night he let me get into Atlas for my peanut butter, bread, and tie-dye shirt. I changed shirts right there, sticking the other one into the pack, and got back into my regular seat.

"Hello everyone, welcome to your nighttime ride around Lake Superior and Huron. Our only stops tonight will be in White River, about four hours from here, and then Sault Ste. Marie, about seven plus hours. My name is Neil, sit back, relax, sleep if you can, and we'll get started."

I took out my jackknife, opened my peanut butter and loaf of rye bread and made a late night snack. Thirty minutes later I fell asleep with my head against the window. Except for a few bumps in the road I didn't wake up until we hit White River, a tiny little town known as the coldest place in Canada.

"You have ten minutes to use the bathroom or have a smoke," said Neil, "This is a quick stop." I quickly walked inside the small building, which was nothing more than a tiny ticket office, four chairs, a cigarette machine, candy machine, and two bathrooms. A couple of passengers stepped off the bus for a smoke before Neil announced it was time to go.

Three hours later, at seven a.m., we entered Sault Ste. Marie. I had slept less than two hours and restlessly at that. My head kept bumping against the bus window and seat back, despite using my flannel shirt as a makeshift pillow. We stopped for twenty minutes as Neil left and Graham took over. It was about an eight hour drive to Niagara Falls, or so I thought. Everyone departed the bus to smoke, use the bathroom, attack the vending machines or because this was their final stop. I could have walked across the International Bridge and the St. Mary's River and been back in the United States. I checked the map inside the station and realized at this point I may as well stick to the bus and ride to Niagara Falls, though the temptation to cross back over to the U.S. was strong. I used the bathroom, washed the night skuz off my face, filled my canteen, and bought a bag of Hostess Hickory Sticks and Dare Maple Leaf cookies from the machines, and a bear claw and black coffee from a Canadian Red Cross fundraising group. Hopefully I was set with food until getting back into the states.

Thirty people got on the bus, including me. I ate my bear claw and drank the coffee while it was still hot. We headed to Sudbury, with a stop in Blind River, Ontario for the customary driver break. Except for the smokers all the passengers stayed on the bus. We continued on for the remaining two hours to Sudbury, making great time, arriving at 10:30 a.m. That's when I discovered I would have to transfer to a new bus in Toronto. Why didn't I know this before, I didn't recall the Regina ticket office clerk telling me that? My mind was mush, I needed sleep, real food, and exercise after twenty-five hours on the bus. The next four hours were spent worrying about getting a new bus from Toronto to the states. This "Express" ride was getting more complicated. I munched on my Maple Leaf cookies to pass time and calm down. The best part was that the bus didn't stop once on the way to the Toronto station.

At the station I was the first person to leave the bus and immediately grabbed Atlas from the baggage handler (Toronto was fancy) and headed to a ticket window. I had to pay an extra ten dollars American for the ticket and by some miracle the bus was leaving in fifteen minutes. What a break. I walked over to the bus and met Gordon, my new driver, who gently put Atlas in the baggage storage area. With my anal side coming out I was surprised and relieved when the third row seat was open, and immediately sat next to the window, spreading my legs out on the other seat making it clear I wanted to stay by myself. I didn't want another drunk joining me. We left the station at eleven a.m. for the two hour ride. It seemed like home was finally within reach.

Michael McCullough

United States

It never occurred to me that Border Patrol would be an issue coming into the states. I was a citizen, lived all my life in the state I was entering, what was the big problem? But here I was being interrogated by Officer Wilson, who had walked onto the bus and was eyeing everyone suspiciously. This was not a trip where police were happy to see me.

"Show me your I.D." I took out my New York driver's license. How about saying please, or hello, or some other polite greeting, a thought I kept in my head.

"New York, yeah, what part, is this your real address?" Man, who tied this asshole's underwear in a knot? Was he related to Officer Mahoney in Utah?

"Brockport, sir, it's about eighty minutes from here, I've lived there all my life," I said.

"So what are you doing in Canada then, how long have you been there?" Wow, what was this prick's problem, was it my tie-dye shirt, my long hair, the two days growth of beard, my bad breath from riding a bus for twenty-nine hours?

"I hitchhiked from Brockport to California, up to Canada and then took a bus back here from Regina."

"Hitchhiked?" he questioned. "Have any drugs on you?"

"What? No, that would be pretty stupid. I have a couple of cookies left, do you want one?"

"What are you, a wise guy? Do you have any luggage in the storage compartment?" Wow, where was Paul's preacher grandfather when you needed him?

"Yes sir, my backpack is in there."

It felt like things were getting pretty serious now. Gordon already had the compartment open and was taking out suitcases and other items, including my pack. Officer Wilson seemed to be enjoying himself tearing through my pack. He didn't care much about where or how things were placed in there; he was determined to find a joint or something to bust me on. Once he realized there were only stinky sneakers, dirty clothes, and little else, he tossed it all on top of Atlas.

"Lucky for you it seems you're clean, pack it all up and get back on the bus."

Officer Wilson seemed disappointed and immediately turned to examine another suitcase. Even though I knew I was clean it was still a nerve wracking experience. I went back on the bus for the short ride across the border to downtown Niagara Falls, New York.

At the station in New York another decision had to be made, do I take another bus, call home for a ride, or get out and hitch? Dad would still be at work and not too excited about a long drive to Niagara Falls and back home, I just didn't feel like hitching at this point, so the bus it was. After the long border stop it was two p.m. This was a busy station. I went to the ticket counter and found out it was only an hour wait for a bus that would take me directly to Brockport and cost five dollars. I quickly bought a ticket and sat down to wait.

The driver, Walter, started stowing our luggage away and let us board at 2:45 p.m. Walter's black Oxford shoes looked like they had been spit polished, his Greyhound shirt and pants freshly ironed, his hair buzzed high and tight like he had just left boot camp, which was unlikely since he looked to be in his thirties.

"How long have you been hauling that pack around?" Walter asked.

"A few weeks, I guess, but not always on a bus. I hitchhiked from Brockport to California, up to Vancouver, then had trouble getting rides and hopped on a bus in Regina."

"Whoa, that's a long trip. You must have had some interesting experiences and, geez, that is one heck of a long bus ride, I drive and aren't sure I'd want to be on a bus that long," said Walter.

"Yeah, I'm a bit tired, even from just riding on the bus. Twenty plus hours is enough. At least you'll get me home to Brockport soon."

"I'll do my best, go get a seat and relax."

I did as Walter told me, and, of course, sat in the third row all by myself.

Walter got on and announced to the twenty or so passengers, "This is the Express bus; our first stop will be in Lockport, then Medina, Albion, and Holley, before finally arriving in Brockport. Hope you enjoy the ride."

Fuck. What is it with these Express buses? I swore never again would I ride an "Express" bus! A ride that would have taken eighty minutes by car took well over two hours, but I was on Main Street in Brockport at five p.m., so overall not too bad. Hitchhiking could have been an all-night ordeal and ended up with me sleeping in another field. But no more buses for me. Ever. What a relief to be back in known territory and only a little over a mile walk from home. I hoisted Atlas onto my back and began the hike when suddenly Paul's older sister, Faith, drove by.

She waved, slowed down, and yelled out the window, "Hey, welcome back to Brockport!" She signaled for me to come over to the car before continuing, "Paul called yesterday; he was in Thunder Bay and hoped to get home tomorrow. He said you two had decided to split up. How long have you been riding a bus?"

I summed up some of my travels by bus as we drove home. Paul lived three houses from me, only a mile from downtown Brockport. Faith non-discreetly kept her window down and stuck her head out like a dog might do. I think my well-worn clothes and body odor had risen to a new level. We pulled into her driveway and Paul's mom came out with her arms crossed and glaring at me, at least that's how I felt.

"Hey Mom, look who I found downtown!" Faith excitedly said.

"Welcome home, Sean, glad you made it safely," Mrs. Davis said dryly.

"Thank you, I'm kind of tired so if you don't mind I'll just go to my house now." It felt like Mrs. Davis was mad at me, maybe for the trip, maybe for splitting with Paul, who knew? She wasn't any friendlier than her parents had been to me back in Seattle. Maybe it was a family trait. Whatever, I didn't have the energy to deal with it. Hey, I didn't make Paul hitchhike across two countries. That was his choice. I was tired, especially after riding on the bus forever, and I really wanted to get home, unpacked, showered, and maybe, if my Mom wasn't pissed too, have something good to eat. I was happy to discover my parents hadn't moved to their new home in Spencerport while I was gone.

Home Again

Dad came home around his usual six p.m. time after working all day at Kodak. He didn't seem too surprised that I was sitting on the living room couch. Maybe Mom had called to warn him about my return. I'd been gone for twenty-five days and it was like I had never left. So weird. Probably internally he was happy I was home, or at least safe, but I began thinking maybe I should have gone off to Alaska with Caleb, took up residence in Colorado, or stayed with Katherine in Brooks.

"When did you get back?" he asked.

"Only an hour ago. Paul and I split up between Calgary and Regina thinking rides would be easier to come by. I made it to Regina, then gave up and took the bus from there to Brockport. It was one long ride, boring, an incredible amount of sitting, of course."

"Did you use the charge card?"

"Yes." Of course that was what he was mainly concerned about, how much money I had spent that was his.

"I owe you for two nights in a hotel, the bus fare, and a small cash advance. Sorry, but of course I'll pay you back as soon as possible. I have some of the money in my bank account and will begin looking for a job."

"Oh, you'll pay me back, no doubt, plus any interest if it's not paid all at once. But it's okay, I'm glad you're back safely and I know you're good for the money. Maybe at dinner you can tell us about the trip. What about Paul, is he back?"

"Not yet. I saw Mrs. Davis; they expect him back tomorrow if he gets a couple decent rides."

"Good, I'm sure they're worried about him," said Dad.

After dinner I emptied Atlas next to the washing machine and spread my tent and sleeping bag out to air on the clothesline in the backyard. It was nice to shower in my own house before going to my bedroom to de-stress and begin to recall some of the things Paul and I had done. I wrote a few pages in my journal about the bus ride while the memories were still fresh.

Before my eyes totally closed for the night I started to think about the next adventure I could take. Unfortunately, getting a job was an immediate concern, and probably would still be a challenge to find something I wouldn't mind going to, but at this point I couldn't be choosy.

Paul did make it home late Friday night. After leaving me he only needed seven rides to make it all the way back home. I guess separating from each other worked out well for him. Maybe I had just been too impatient about waiting for rides. If I hadn't been left so late at night at that strip mall in Regina and been able to find a decent place to sleep, who knows, there may have been no need to ride the bus.

Paul shared some of his experiences with me Saturday night while we were walking to the Barge Inn; "Yeah, Sean, I guess I got lucky. My first ride took me all the way to Winnipeg. I tried to get the driver to pick you up too, but he refused, he felt scared having two strangers in the car. He turned out to be a pretty nice guy, invited me to stay the night and sleep on the living room floor.

In the morning he dropped me off at the on-ramp to Highway 1 on his way to work. After a couple of hours I scored again, getting another long ride, this time to Sudbury. I slept in a park off of Highway 1, it wasn't too bad though. I had soft grass for my sleeping bag and the bathroom was open all night. In the morning it took two rides to get to Mississauga, a bit south of Toronto, where I stayed another night, unfortunately having to sleep in a small park on a picnic table. Actually that was a bit scary, lots of traffic nearby and a few other people wandering around the park during the night. I had a pretty restless night of trying to sleep. At sunrise I immediately went to the highway and waited about two hours before getting a ride from some salesman going to Niagara Falls. He let me out on Route 104 and I needed only two more rides to get to Brockport around nine p.m. It didn't work out too bad for me, I guess, a bit lonely, but interesting nonetheless. How about you, Faith said you ended up on a bus from Regina?"

I told him my story about staying in Regina and the difficult decision to begin the long, miserable ride on the "Express Bus" as we walked the two miles from our homes to the Barge Inn. It was a warm, humid, typical late July Brockport night and we arrived just in time for Scott to pour our first happy hour drinks. The boys were back in town. For now.

"Would you tell me please, which way I ought to go from here?" (Carroll, 71)

THE END

Epilogue

The immediate future seemed easy for Paul, he was the type of person who was zeroed in on his goals. He was entering his junior year and couldn't wait to get started. The Monday after arriving back in Brockport Paul began working out in the college weight room, doing sprints on the football field, and running repeats up and down the stadium bleachers. Paul cut back on his drinking and purchased his course textbooks in early August to get a head start on geology classes.

To his credit Paul tried to convince me that going out for football was the right thing to do. My weight may have been low, but I could try linebacker, or special teams, who knew? I kept him company in the weight room, but didn't have the drive to want to practice and get hit, or hit someone, every day.

Instead, in late August, I enrolled at Brockport State for the fall semester. At this point in my life it seemed the right thing to do. The blank journals I had purchased from Scrantom's Books & Stationery store in Rochester were getting full as I recorded the experiences of our hitchhiking trip. I registered for classes in creative writing, American lit I, historical geology, writing in the earth sciences, and air & water pollution. Soon after getting home I mailed my film cartridges to Kodak for processing, but it was going to take three weeks for them to be ready to pick up.

Lucky for me the owner of the Barge Inn had decided to rent space next door to the bar and open a delicatessen and sub shop. I began working a couple of nights and some weekends at the deli, and, eventually, was able to earn enough money to pay back Dad and for my college books, tuition, and partying.

Ultimately, I was able to focus a little better on my classes than in previous semesters. But I did continue playing as many pickup basketball games as I could, and working out in the weight room, while dreaming of my next adventure. Staying in motion, that's what life was all about.

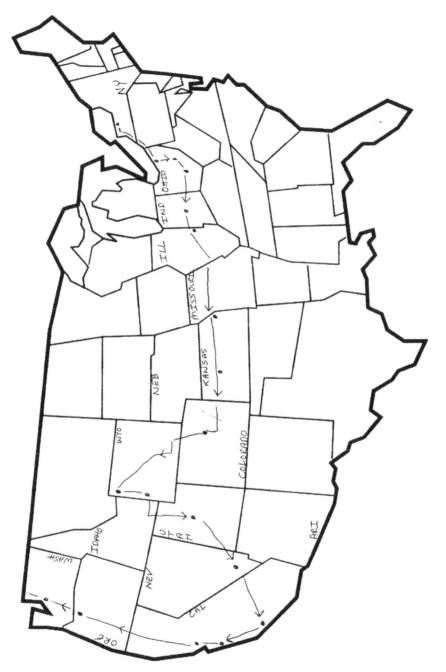

Route across the United States.

[7] Jones, Bruce, "US and Canada Printable, Blank Maps, "Royalty Free US and World Maps, 2010-2019, www.freeusaandworldmaps.com.

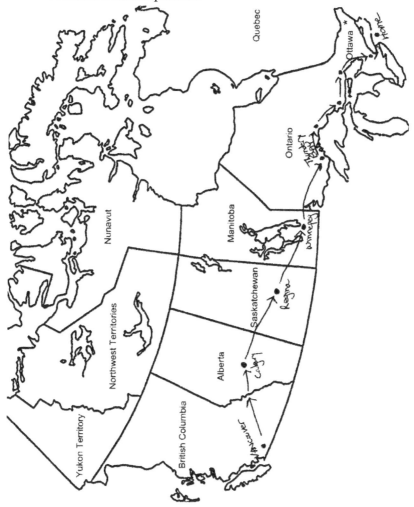

Route across Canada.
[8] (Jones).

Michael McCullough

About the Author

Michael McCullough has experience hitchhiking but decided it was best to stop many years ago when he was young and had hair. He still refuses to ride on an "Express" bus. Michael prefers drinking Bourbon or Irish whiskey now instead of rum. Recently retired, he spent years working as a children's, middle school, and college librarian. He earned his Bachelor of Science Degree in Earth Science from SUNY at Brockport and Masters in Library Science degree from the University at Buffalo.

Michael has had many book and website reviews published in School Library Journal and Choice. He wrote dozens of library guides for student and professor use at a local community college. Michael designed a middle school library website and wrote content for several years. He also wrote content for blogs about libraries, running, and triathlons.

He is married and has three daughters and one granddaughter.

Michael is a long time runner and triathlete. He still wakes up in the middle of the night dreaming of playing professional football or becoming an astronaut.

This is his first novel.

<u>Starry Night Publishing</u>

Everyone has a story...

Don't spend your life trying to get published! Don't tolerate rejection! Don't do all the work and allow the publishing companies to reap the rewards!

Millions of independent authors like you are making money, publishing their stories now. Our technological know-how will take the headaches out of getting published. Let Starry Night Publishing take care of the hard parts, so you can focus on writing. You simply send us your Word Document, and we do the rest. It really is that simple!

The big companies want to publish only "celebrity authors," not the average book-writer. It's almost impossible for first-time authors to get published today. This has led many authors to go the self-publishing route. Until recently, this was considered "vanity-publishing." You spent large sums of your money to get twenty copies of your book, to give to relatives at Christmas just so you could see your name on the cover. However, the self-publishing industry allows authors to get published in a timely fashion, retain the rights to your work, keeping up to ninety percent of your royalties instead of the traditional five percent.

We've opened up the gates, allowing you inside the world of publishing. While others charge you as much as fifteen-thousand dollars for a publishing package, we charge less than five-hundred dollars to cover copyright, ISBN, and distribution costs. Do you really want to spend all your time formatting, converting, designing a cover, and then promoting your book because no one else will?

Our editors are professionals, able to create a top-notch book that you will be proud of. Becoming a published author is supposed to be fun, not a hassle.

At Starry Night Publishing, you submit your work, we create a professional-looking cover, a table of contents, compile your text and images into the appropriate format, convert your files for eReaders, take care of copyright information, assign an ISBN, allow you to keep one-hundred-percent of your rights, distribute your story worldwide on Amazon, Barnes and Noble and many other retailers, and write you a check for your royalties. There are no other hidden fees involved! You don't pay extra for a cover or to keep your book in print. We promise! Everything is included! You even get a free copy of your book and unlimited half-price copies.

In nine short years, we've published more than four thousand books, compared to the major publishing houses, which only add an average of six new titles per year. We will publish your fiction or non-fiction books about anything and look forward to reading your stories and sharing them with the world.

We sincerely hope that you will join the growing Starry Night Publishing family, become a published author, and gain the world-wide exposure that you deserve. You deserve to succeed. Success comes to those who make opportunities happen, not those who wait for opportunities to happen. You just have to try. Thanks for joining us on our journey.

www.starrynightpublishing.com

www.facebook.com/starrynightpublishing/

Made in the USA
Middletown, DE
12 October 2021